CHEAP THRILLS

JESSE PULLINS

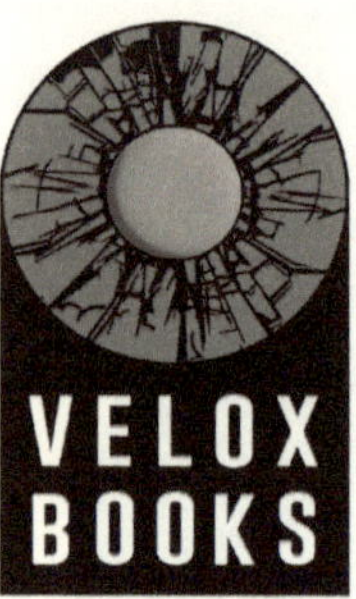

Published by arrangement with the author.

The story, all names, characters, and incidents portrayed in this production are fictitious. No identification with actual persons (living or deceased), places, buildings, and products is intended or should be inferred.

YOU'RE READING ANOTHER TERRIFYING COLLECTION FROM

**FOLLOW VELOX TO KEEP
THE NIGHTMARES COMING:**

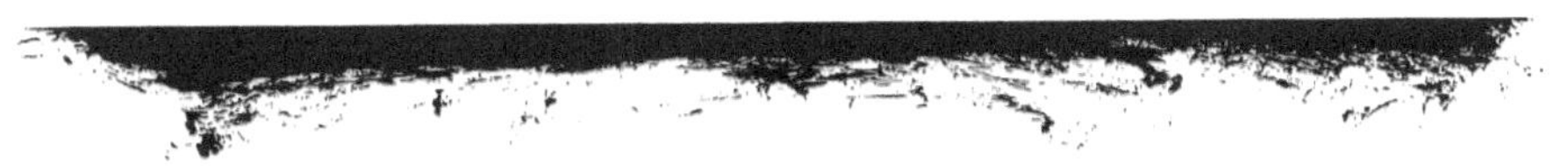

For my wife, who has been there every step of the way. You are my backbone, my rock, and this would have been impossible without you. Forever and always.

CONTENTS

A DOCTOR'S VISIT

Wesley counted the ceiling tiles as he waited. He already knew how many there were, one hundred thirteen to be exact, but for some reason, he always felt like he missed one. Every time he counted the tiles, he always felt like he jumped to the next tile in a row too quickly and skipped one. Several times, he had started from the beginning just to make sure he would get it right, but he would always get discouraged when he thought he skipped that one t ile.

Sometimes he wondered why he continued to count them after all this time. They never changed; the tiles had remained the same since the day his mother brought him in for the very first time, when he was an infant. Of course, he couldn't recollect how they looked since he was a baby, but he *assumed* they had never changed. Now, at thirty-five, Wesley found himself counting the same damn tiles, waiting on the same general practitioner, Dr. Sobieski. The tiles were faded yellow with age, like an old, dusty book that had been kept in the attic for a little too long. The same thing could be said about the doctor.

Aside from the faded tiles and depressed carpet, it had hardly changed since he was a kid, back when counting tiles was a necessity. The same simple glassed-in receptionist desk and nine lobby chairs to sit in that formed a 'U' shape, with an end table in each corner that was always littered with shitty magazines—National Geographic from the early 2000s, five years' worth of *People*. Things didn't get much better for Dr. Sobieski's patients until about four years ago, when he installed a tube TV/VCR combo in the upper corners of the room.

Whether it was Sobieski's attempt at modernization or an act of mercy from one of the receptionists, Wesley didn't know. Only one thing was certain: *somebody* was using it to cycle their private collection of *Disney* films. Even now, Wesley watched as Scar dug his claws into Mufasa for the hundredth time, before letting him plummet into the rampaging stampede of wildebeests. Even as an adult, it was painful to watch.

The angle of the television was straining his injured neck. He looked away, rubbing it lightly with his hand. He hoped it was nothing too severe. He was probably fine.

Earlier that afternoon, while out mudding, he lost control and flipped his four-wheeler. He thought for sure in the instant the ATV pinned him that he was a broken man—the handlebars pressed against his throat so tight that he thought his eyes would burst out of his skull. When his brothers pulled the four-wheeler off him and he got up and walked, he thought it was a miracle. If it weren't for his wife's pestering, he wouldn't be here in the first place. After all, he was only a little sore, like he had pulled a muscle or two in his neck, just tweaked it a little bit. Other than that, he just got a nasty scrape on the inside of his thigh, right in the meat of it. Nothing a good night's sleep and a day off work couldn't solve. The bruises would heal, and he'd feel better in no time.

But his wife wouldn't have any of it. Meryl had made the appointment before she left for work, and said they could "squeeze" him in.

"You're getting older," she had stated bluntly, "better safe than sorry."

He knew she meant well, but still. Sitting in the empty waiting room, counting the tiles while Simba screamed. He could be two beers in by now with his feet up.

Wesley's pride kept him from hitching a ride to the doctor. His brothers understood his stubbornness and let him man up, but not without tailing him to the office to make sure he got there in one piece. When he arrived, they coached him to call if there was anything major. They had each experienced their own nasty wrecks, each time emerging victorious with scars to brag about. The Porter boys were known to be reckless and lucky. He almost felt it was his duty not to be a girl about it and see the doc to ease Meryl's concern. Sometimes she worried too much. At least this way it saved him from the ass-chewing he would receive for not listening to her.

Just as he was about to ask the receptionist how much longer it would take, she poked her head out of her booth and called, "Mr. Porter?"

"Yes, ma'am." He rose from his chair a little too quickly, and the nasty ache prodded his neck. He grit his teeth and straightened his posture, collecting himself quickly before following her.

"Let's get you weighed up before he sees you," she said, smiling her plastic smile. Dr. Sobieski's girls were always polite. Too bad you could always tell when they were faking it. Cheerily staring daggers over the fact that they were kept over an extra half hour because somebody's neck was sore.

Wesley walked slowly out of the waiting room and into the hallway. He was groggy and out of it from the wreck, almost like he was hungover. A throbbing headache resided behind his eyes, and his limbs felt like broken boards. Every step he took made him wish he were just lying in bed, buried underneath a thick layer of blankets so he could fall asleep and forget about the pain.

You're getting older, he thought.

Wesley feigned a smile and continued on like it was nothing to worry about. The Porter boys didn't get hurt; they just had fun.

When he arrived at the dusty scale, the nurse instructed him to remove his boots and step on. He unlaced them quickly, ignoring the aches that were starting to spread. Was he just coming down with the flu? It was a struggle to keep his back straight, but he kept his head held high while she toyed with the counterweights to get an accurate measurement.

"Two... thirty-eight," she said at last, jotting the weight down on her clipboard. It was about ten more than he hoped.

Wesley stepped off the scale and grabbed his boots, the nurse already walking away.

"Alright, dear, let's get you in a room so the doctor can see you," she instructed, not even facing him, leading him to a room on the far left of the hallway. He didn't know why she was taking him to a room so far away. There was nobody else in the waiting room, and he was almost positive he was the only patient at this hour. A visit to Dr. Sobieski's was known to take forever; whether it was the young nurses that kept him or just his old age, Wesley didn't know. When he was a kid, he would often fall asleep before the doctor got to him. Back in the day, it was a good way to pass the time, instead of looking at the same childish charts of the human skeleton or the maps of muscle tissue that always seemed to freak him out. Too bad he was too old to pull such a thing—he felt like he could use a nap now.

The nurse led him into the room and had him sit on the examination table. The thin paper covering the leather crackled and tore when he sat down, just like it did every other time he had to sit on the benches. It made him smile. Three decades, and they were still using the same shit that made the same noise. You'd think they would've come up with a better way to keep the thing "sanitary".

Once seated, she began the expected barrage of questions.

"Can you verify your name and birthday for me?"

"What brings you in today?"

"Describe how it happened to me."

"Does it hurt to move it?"

"Any loss of vision or feeling disoriented?"

"On a scale of one to ten, ten being the worst pain imaginable, how bad does it hurt?"

He responded: "Uh... a five."

Any other time, he would've been able to answer all the questions quickly, even make jokes out of it. In truth, the more times he tried to recollect the accident, the fuzzier it became. Each time he replayed the wreck, it felt like it just fast-forwarded to the bars on his neck. It had happened so fast. He summed it up the best he could.

He was going a little too fast on his four-wheeler and caught more air than expected when he jumped a muddy trench in the woods behind his brother's house. He thought he was prepared for the initial landing, but at the last second, he noticed a large log in his path and hit it head-on once he landed. The quad flipped forward, tossing him over the handlebars with the ATV tumbling after him. Wesley rolled several feet. He remembered getting scraped by the rocky earth and struck by a stray branch on his thigh. The stick must have punctured his leg or something, but he couldn't quite remember. With some miracle (or luck), he got up, walked, and was able to drive to the doctor's office.

The nurse scrawled everything quickly while nodding along, before moving on to take his temperature, with the thermometer wedged under his tongue. Wesley sat there patiently with the metal probe jutting out of his mouth. It was uncomfortable, the way the rod stabbed under his tongue. It was a relief when she retrieved it. She informed him that he had a temp of 99.3, slightly elevated, but nothing drastic. She asked him if he felt nauseous. After a "no," she moved on to blood pressure.

The rip of the Velcro was loud in the small room, and the tough fabric of the sleeve felt strange to his skin while the nurse fastened the cuff right under his armpit. Wesley had always thought the act of checking blood pressure was unusual, and in this day and age, it was still a common practice to inflate the tube with a small black rubber pump. With every squeeze, the sleeve constrict-ed around his bicep, squeezing almost too tightly like it always did. He felt the odd panic in his gut when the inflation reached its peak, like his arm would sever from the rest of his body. The veins in his arm bulged, and he felt the lack of circulation and the pulse of his heart through the entire limb.

"Your blood pressure is 130 over 86. Somebody needs to lay off the beer and brats," the nurse joked, before removing the cuff. The blood returning to his fingers was uncomfortable. He didn't know what put him off more, the unnatural sensation in his arm, or the nurse's remark. Why did she specifically mention those two? Did she think all grown men feasted on brats and guzzled down beers every chance they had? More importantly, how did she guess so accurately?

He forced a chuckle while she hung everything up and made way for the door. She told him that the doctor would be with him shortly. Wesley breathed a sigh of relief and slowly stretched out on the exam table. His neck felt like it was getting stiffer. His whole body felt like creaking lumber. The scrape on his thigh itched annoyingly, and he tried to scratch it through the denim of his jeans. After a couple of scratches, he felt a pain so startling it made his leg jolt.

Wesley cursed, thinking maybe he had picked away a scab. From then on, he left his leg alone, letting the itch continue despite how much it made him uncomfortable.

The minutes dragged on as Wesley waited for the doctor to arrive. Although it wasn't as excruciating as he remembered. The longer he lay on the crackling paper, the more comfortable he became. He felt drowsy. He looked at his feet hanging over the bed, swinging back and forth the way they did when he was younger. He looked at one of the stirrups jutting from the side of the table and nudged it with his foot. It squeaked loudly, making him jump. He laughed nervously. Why was he feeling so skittish? Goosebumps crawled up his arms, like a chill had drifted in. When his eyes grew heavy, he found himself giving in. He felt so *fatigued.* It had to be the flu.

The doorknob turned, and his eyes shot open, just as Dr. Sobieski opened the door. He was already adjusting his glasses to get a better look at the chart, not even looking his direction as he let the door drift closed behind him.

"How are we feeling today, Mr. Porter? Took a little tumble, I hear." Each word was spoken slowly, weathered by age. He flipped through the chart, beady little eyes scanning the paperwork behind thick, bifocal glasses.

Wesley chuckled in embarrassment and rubbed sheepishly at his neck.

"Yeah, Doc. I never saw that log coming," he said. The same feeling of deja vu crept over him every time he had this kind of conversation with Sobieski. This had to have been the tenth time they'd had a conversation similar to this. Always something reckless, but never anything too serious.

"Uh-huh. You know, Wesley, I don't know what to do with you boys. Some day, one of you is going to come in here with a bump on the head, and it will be out of my hands. But I've been telling you guys that for years."

There was that smug little grin on his face. It was grandfatherly, like he was scolding one of his own. Wesley couldn't describe why it was comforting.

"Well, you know what they say about us, Doc. We're invincible," he told him, but something felt different about this time. The soreness he was experiencing was different. Wesley chalked it up to old age and becoming a worrywart just like his Meryl.

Sobieski set the chart down and reached for his stethoscope.

"I sure hope so. Let's have a look at you, son."

The doctor reached into Wesley's shirt and pressed the cool metal to his chest. The same old instructions ensued; he could probably sing along with him. Breathe in, breathe out. Take a deep breath now, hold it, and then exhale. One more time for me.

"You sound tired. Stay up too late partying, I presume?" The doctor asked.

In truth, he was tired. But there was no partying last night, just work, dinner, TV, and sleep. Nothing out of the ordinary.

"Nah, just another day. Prolly' just tired from the quad, I guess. I mowed this morning, so there's that, too."

The eye exam was next. Dr. Sobieski had him trace the tiny glow of a pen light, left to right, up and down. The doctor gazed into his retinas, as if he were staring into the clockwork of a wristwatch. Wesley always wondered what he was looking for, what he saw. Maybe he'd never know.

After that, it was the semi-uncomfortable ear check. This was the part that always made Wesley chuckle on the inside. Ever since he was a child, when Sobieski examined his ears, he told him he was growing potatoes in them. Today was no exception.

Once that was done, the doctor wanted to have a look at his neck. He delicately inspected it with gloved hands, asking him question after question while he did so. So tell me again how this happened? Does this hurt? Does it hurt to walk? Do you feel any kind of discomfort? Describe to me how you fell. Do you have any other injuries I should be concerned about?

Dr. Sobieski noted there was a slight bruising on his neck. It was in a light "V" shape around the entire front of his neck where the handlebars had pinned him.

Wesley described how the accident happened, what he could recollect and how he landed. It was getting exhausting. He tried to be as thorough as possible, but at the end of it all, he just rolled his fucking quad in the mud, and it pinned him down. It was somewhat challenging to provide a play-by-play. On account of another injury, he said the only thing he could recall specifically was the scrape on his inner thigh, from a branch or brush—whatever it had been.

"Just to be sure it's nothing serious, we're going to have you get an X-ray immediately. I'll have Cindy prep, and we'll get it taken care of. She'll come get you when we're ready for you. You're going to have to strip and put on the paper gown," He reached into the bottom drawer of the cabinet next to him and pulled one that was neatly folded in plastic wrap, before concluding, "I know how much you love those."

Wesley scowled at the thought of it. This was getting drawn out more than he'd hoped. He was ready to go home and put some ice on it, put his feet up.

Sobieski departed, and Wesley got undressed. It took him longer than expected, every muscle stiff and sore to the point he just wanted to lie down. By the time he got down to his boxers, he was drained, spending the last of the energy he had to kick his clothes into a little pile by the examination table. He thought about texting Meryl to let her know how it was going, but decided not to. The thought of the effort it would take to get his phone felt daunting.

"We're ready for you in X-ray, Mr. Porter. Please come this way." Cindy held the door open and motioned for him to follow.

Wesley gave a slight nod and followed, feeling awkward in the paper gown. Luckily, there was nobody around, and he didn't have to suffer further embarrassment. But as he made his way down the hall, there didn't seem to be anyone else in sight. From the looks of it, it seemed like the only ones left were Cindy and the Doc. Everyone else must have left for the night.

The X-ray room was dark. The only lighting came from the overhead lamp on the radiography table and the glow from the computer monitor inside the little room where the doctor stands.

"Go ahead and have a seat, dear," Cindy said.

Wesley climbed onto the table and rolled onto his back, the dim room feeling heavy. He could now see Dr. Sobieski through the glass, the monitor's glow giving him a faint silhouette, his bi-focals reflecting the screen's light. Cindy adjusted the lamp for the appropriate angle, and he watched the yellow glow shift across his body until it rested uncomfortably on his face. With squinted eyes, he felt Cindy lay the lead vest on top of him, immediately feeling like he was being smothered. The weight of the vest made him want to sleep, but the glaring light kept him awake.

"Just going to take a couple of pictures here, try your best to lie still." Sobieski's voice crackled over the intercom, and Wesley obliged. He was too tired to move; he just wanted to lie there.

Wesley's breathing felt loud under the vest, and the whir of the machine consumed the room. He thought maybe he would even take the day off work tomorrow and try to rest. He couldn't remember the last time he missed work.

There was a faint clicking sound as the machine took its pictures, and before he knew it, the lights were back on. Wesley couldn't explain *why*, but things felt like they were going too fast.

Sobieski was next to him now, placing a hand on his shoulder, already speaking.

"All I'll need is a moment to look these over to make sure everything's alright. I'll have Cindy take you back to your room, and you can get dressed. We'll have you on your way in no time, son. How do you feel?" he asked.

"Tired. Sore. Ready to go home," Wesley said. In truth, he felt a little lightheaded, but he chalked it up to the change in lighting.

"I bet. It's not every day somebody gets buried under an ATV. Everything looks good so far, though, you Porter boys are tough eggs to crack. Cindy," he motioned to the nurse, and with a farewell, gave Wesley's shoulder a pat.

The doctor departed, and the nurse asked if he needed help getting up. Wesley refused. He wanted to keep his pride intact. But it took much more effort getting up than it did lying down, and Wesley struggled slightly to stand straight. The nurse hovered with uncertainty, but he waved her away.

They were walking down the hall now, the nurse in front, the clipboard at her hip. She was going over what he should do when he got home, speaking aloud without turning to look at him. Wesley was trying to listen, but couldn't quite hear her. Not only did he suddenly feel sick to his stomach, but there was now an incredible soreness in his shoulder. He rubbed it with his hand, trying to soothe the aching muscles, but the motion hurt him. He couldn't help but think it was the same place Dr. Sobieski had his hand.

They arrived at his room, the nurse still talking about how he should take it easy and use plenty of ice. Something about a prescription to ease the pain and how a doctor's note wouldn't be a problem. She told him he could get dressed, and the doctor would return to review his X-rays in a moment.

After a mumble of acknowledgement, Cindy left Wesley sitting on the examination table, the door once again shut behind her. Wesley looked at the pile of clothes by his feet, trying to muster up the energy to put them back on. He was beginning to feel very nauseous and top-heavy. It took more effort than necessary to move, and when he knelt down to grab his pants off the floor, he felt like he had been hit by a truck. His breathing was labored, like each inhale was struggling through a straw. With his hand only inches away from his clothes, he retreated to the examination table to rest and catch his breath.

He didn't feel like himself. Everything felt *wrong*.

There was a quick knock on the door followed by the entry of Dr. Sobieski, his own clipboard under his arm, while he focused on the film held out in front of him.

"Good news, Mr. Porter, nothing's broken. The whiplash from your accident must have taken quite a toll on you, but there is no visible damage to any vertebrae. I'm going to need you to get plenty of—" Sobieski stopped suddenly, his eyes narrowing in at something on the film. He had a confused, almost baffled look on his face. He adjusted his glasses and brought it in closer, staring intensely.

"What in god's name..." he mumbled to himself, making Wesley incredibly nervous.

"Doc, something's not right. I, uh, I don't feel so good," he mumbled, each word barely escaping his lips. The room was starting to spin slowly, like a merry-go-round idling in the wind.

Dr. Sobieski briefly tore his gaze from the x-ray to look at Wesley, examining him and referring to the film several times. The doctor looked very unsure, like he didn't know what he was looking at. The more he studied the clipboard, the more he looked physically uncomfortable, nervously scratching his head. Without a word, he took a small step backwards towards the door, his hand already reaching for the knob.

"W-wait here just a minute, Mr. Porter. I-I need to check something real quick. Don't go anywhere," he stammered and pulled the door open, disappearing before Wesley could say anything else.

The door slammed shut behind him immediately, followed by the click of the knob's lock.

"Wait, Doc, I don't feel—" Wesley sputtered, lacking the energy to say any more. Every muscle in his body burned, and his head throbbed with each beat of his heart. His brain felt like it was trying to force its way out of his skull. He held his head with shaking hands, feeling like he'd fall over. The earth felt like it was moving too fast beneath his feet.

Wesley looked at the floor, measuring the distance between his feet and the tile. He wanted to get his clothes back on and get the fuck out of there. Taking his time, he braced himself on the examination table and reached out to the floor with his feet. The throbbing in his head made it nearly impossible to focus, but he tried his best to concentrate. He inched his toes forward, slowly and steadily, waiting for his digits to touch the cool floor. Harnessing everything he had, he touched the tile; his toes first, then the pads of his feet, followed by the heels. He was standing now. Just the small feat was enough to give him relief. He could do this. Now all he needed to do was get dressed.

Wesley steadied himself again, looked down at his clothes, and puked all over them.

The bile regurgitated out of nowhere, and Wesley found himself bracing the table again while he heaved uncontrollably. His body succumbed to the nausea like a valve had been broken loose.

His abs contracted violently, so hard he thought his stomach was being ripped apart. Wesley's legs felt weak, and they shook under the growing weight of the rest of his body. After a final purge, he opened his eyes and was horrified at what he saw.

Splashed all over his clothes and the floor surrounding them was blood, mixed with some kind of meaty chunks that resembled shredded raw steak. The sight of the horror made him dizzy, and his legs failed him. He watched himself plummet to the floor through waves of in-and-out darkness, like everything was happening seconds before he could react.

Wesley landed on his back, his right leg slipping and kicking his clothes while his left bent with his knee pointing to the ceiling. If his head bounced off the floor, he couldn't tell in the midst of all the things that ailed him.

"Doc!" Wesley yelled as he lay feebly on the floor, his vision scattered. His stomach churned with what felt like raw acid, and each time he tried to get up, it felt like he was being pummeled. Every muscle, every joint burned with an electric pain so fierce it paralyzed him.

"Help me! Please!" His voice sounded winded and broken. Through the constant torture, Wesley felt a different sensation, not in his head or stomach but in his leg. It was a tingling kind of feeling, but it itched and he didn't have the energy anymore to scratch it. All he could do now was look. He watched in disbelief as his inner left thigh bulged under the skin, and a tiny twisting shape fought to get out. The teardrop-shaped outline pressed against the inside of his skin so persistently that it split the membrane, blood spurting as it was bored from the inside.

"What the fuck—" Wesley screamed deliriously. The hole in his leg split wider, and a tiny pair of circular teeth *chewed* their way through, squirming to the surface. It was the shape of a slug but had large, bulbous eyes and a small mouth housing dozens of dagger-like teeth, like a lamprey.

The larval-like organism slithered a few inches down his leg, and did what he could only describe as *stare* at him. A whining noise emitted from the terrifying creature, like a whistling teapot on a red-hot burner. Its slimy body expanded, puffing up below its mouth as if taking in a large breath of fresh air. Wesley watched through watering eyes, speechless. Suddenly, the whining ceased, and the slug exploded, showering the room in a sticky red mess.

What is happening to me fucking slug monster came out of my leg. Am I dying? I just want to go home—

Wesley heard voices outside the door, and he tried his best to concentrate through the pounding in his skull. There were several of them—Dr. Sobieski's and others that he did not recognize, *firmer* voices. Finally, they were coming to help him. Now they would give him some kind of explanation, telling him how they were going to fix him and everything would be okay, and he would be home soon.

It took everything he had to get off his back. His palms burned like they were smothered in fiberglass. He focused on the blood and meat covering his clothes. It brought a sense of impending doom, the reality that it hadn't been *food* that came up. In the back of his mind, he felt it wasn't going to be okay. Even though every cell in his body told him otherwise, he still hoped to God there was some way he would go home to his wife, and she would hold him in her arms.

So Wesley sat and stared at the door, his breath coming in heaves. Tears streamed through the fresh blood spatter on his face. He was scared and panicking. He found himself glancing at his wedding ring, wishing his wife were there to comfort him. He could see the gold glinting through the red. The cursive writing is inscribed in the ring.

Even if he couldn't, he knew the words by heart. "Forever and Always" had been etched in the gold, matching the inscription on the sterling diamond ring that Meryl wore. He wanted her to know that he loved her. He wanted to tell her, to see her one last time, if it was the last thing he did.

There was a knock at the door, followed by the immediate entry of three men. What looked like two policemen were first, Dr. Sobieski reluctantly behind them. With just a glance at their vests and guns, Wesley could feel the downward spiral.

"Mr. Porter?" Sobieski called out, entering slowly. He held his clipboard to his chest, his eyes suddenly widening at the mess. The officers scanned the room, instantly repulsed by what they saw. One of them covered their nose as if to ward off some stench, the other reflexively resting his hand on his gun.

"Jesus Christ," one of them mumbled. The other already had a hand resting on the gun that was holstered at his hip. The gesture made Wesley extremely uncomfortable.

"What's... going on, Doc? There's... something... *wrong* with me. I... need... help." Wesley struggled with every word. His heart pulsed erratically in his chest. His gaze shifted from the frightened doctor to the apprehensive officers.

"I'm afraid there's something terribly wrong with you, Wesley. Something I can't explain. These men are here to take you to where you can get help. An ambulance is on the way. They'll find out what's wrong. I'm sorry, son." Sobieski said solemnly, avoiding eye contact with the patient whom he had tended to for over thirty years. The bigger of the two officers stepped forward, one hand slowly pulling the cuffs from his belt.

"I don't... understand. I want... go home..." Wesley tried to scoot himself away, but his hand just slid on the bloody tile.

Cautiously stepping around him, the officer readied the handcuffs while the other started to flank him, stepping around the mess. When the one with the cuffs got behind him, the chained bracelets jingled as he reached for one of Wesley's arms.

"They're going to find out what's wrong with you, son. Just cooperate, and it'll be okay. I'm sorry it had to come to this," The doctor repeated, maintaining a safe distance while the policemen took over. He was sweating, and there was a fear in his eyes unlike anything Wesley had ever seen.

The officer laid a rugged grip on his arm and hauled him up so fast that his legs buckled and slipped. Wesley didn't understand what was happening. He couldn't comprehend why the police were here and why they were taking him into custody. He did nothing wrong. Just before the first cuff was clasped around his wrist, Wesley started to resist, devoting what little energy he had left to thwart what was transpiring.

"No! Get... off me!" He shouted and stumbled, alarming the police as he tried to pull away. The doctor backed away in fear, and the officer in front prepared to restrain him. The man behind him strengthened his iron grip on Wesley's arm, but he somehow slipped out of his hold.

The officer looked at his hand, seeing nothing but a gory sleeve of skin clutched in his grasp, pulled straight from the raw muscle. It had ripped away like paper.

"What the fuck—" The man gasped, shaking it free from his grasp. It hit the tile with a wet *plap*.

The officer in front of Wesley gripped his gown in both of his thick hands, balling it up in fists as he tried to snatch him up. Wesley tried to push him away, his hands weakly pressing against the man's large frame. His palm connected with the officer's shoulder, just past the protection of the Kevlar. He instantly reared back, yelping in pain as he clutched his shoulder, blood oozing through his fingers like he was suffering from a gunshot.

Wesley was just as surprised and looked at his hand as if some sort of miracle had transpired. Sticking out of his palm was a barb, about two inches in length, round at the base but filed to a point like a thorn from a rosebush. He felt a numbness in his hands, like a trickle of morphine was creeping up his arm. Where the skin had been ripped from his other arm, he felt nothing aside from the sensation of blood running down the limb.

Between the wound in his shoulder and Wesley's mutilated arm, the police officer began to panic and barked at the other.

"Hit him!"

Wesley heard the crackle of electricity immediately, the undeniable ticking of a taser arc. A second later, his already diminishing world turned to hell. The cop held the taser to Wesley's lower back, shooting fifty thousand volts into his lower lumbar. The jolt was like an injected thunderstorm. His arms and legs contorted into locked positions, and his body convulsed, but he did not fall. Even as his mouth frothed and his eyes felt like bursting for the second time for the day, his bare feet remained rooted to the tile like anchors.

"NO... STOP!" Wesley screamed through the paralyzing volts. His teeth rattled from the amperage. They vibrated so much he felt his molars would pop like popcorn.

Dr. Sobieski was traumatized. He cowered in the corner, one arm clinging to the clipboard while the other shielded his face from the brutality. He didn't want to see the tears in his eyes, the foam from his mouth, the bloody shedding of skin.

Through the shock, Wesley felt a transformation overtake him. Watching through the teary eyes, he witnessed his contorted wrists *break* downward, the skin and muscle tearing as his hands were forced to bend unnaturally. His middle and ring fingers felt a similar alteration. The digits cracked and separated, doubling in length as they extended far past his other fingers. Each tip of the slender appendages ripped at the tips, cuticles and fingernails falling away in the wake of jagged bone claws.

"God help us..." Dr. Sobieski wailed, eyes wild with terror as he watched what Wesley was becoming.

The officers shouted menacingly. The injured one pulled his sidearm and grabbed at the gown once more, training the weapon inches from Wesley's face. Wesley was screaming now, the tendons in his neck stretched taut as his body was mutilated from the inside.

The officer in the rear hit him with the taser again, turning up the voltage to subdue him, but it proved unsuccessful.

Wesley felt a churning in his gut that soon turned to stabbing, and he gagged as a swirling mass was working its way up his throat. It squirmed and raked against his insides, and he dry-heaved repeatedly through the paralyzing shock of the taser. Wesley's mouth opened wide as the slithering projection arrived on his tongue, and the police officer yelled in fear when he saw the pair of razor teeth slice through Wesley's cheeks. An alien mandible jutted from his mouth, and a vertical set of pincer teeth snapped wildly between his jaws.

The cop raised his Glock and fired twice into Wesley's chest. The bullets drilled through the flesh but ricocheted off something internally. Wesley lurched forward and latched the jaws' teeth onto the officer's face, piercing the temples on both sides of his head. Each large pincer dug deep into his skull in a deadly guillotine motion. The screaming became irate and broken, and the officer squeezed off rounds rapidly, the pistol bucking out of control as bullets tore through the doctor's office.

One of the hollow-points struck Wesley's left cheekbone, obliterating part of his face and revealing a heavily stained chartreuse exoskeleton. The mandible squeezed until it sheared through the skull, severing the officer's head cleanly, releasing a torrent of crimson in the tight room. The body of the officer slumped heavily to the floor, and the portion containing only eyes and a hairline rolled away.

A heavy, metallic scent pervaded the air, and Sobieski shuddered as his stark white coat faded to a deep red. The officer behind him yelped in fear, staggering back and colliding with the examination table.

Wesley felt immediate relief at the taser's release. His morphing body went slack as the electric shock ceased, and he regained a taller, more oppressive stature. The bones in his body were shifting, one after another to accommodate his newly found form. The skin on his body hung loosely, revealing a spiked bony husk pressing from beneath. Several black spines protruded from his forearms, making him a walking iron maiden. The pain in his body had succumbed entirely to the numbness, and even as twig-like arms penetrated his rib cage and parted his gown, he felt nothing but a newfound, primal adrenaline—a *rage.* The thin arms flailed through the air, newborn fingers cracking as they flexed.

"This is Officer Brant calling for backup! I repeat, Officer Brant requesting—"

Wesley spun around and snatched the radio, his hand moving in one quick motion, crushing the hardware and tendons together like crushed aluminum can. Officer Brant screamed and jabbed at him with the stun gun, the sparking tip arcing repeatedly as he tried to zap him again. Time seemed to move more slowly for Wesley, each movement from his assailant easily anticipated. The arms sticking from his abdomen snatched the stun gun away and broke it in two like a plastic toy, and tossed the useless hardware to the floor.

Officer Brant reached for his baton but stopped short when Wesley raised a hooked raptorial arm and brought it down in a blur, impaling him above the collar bone with his jagged fingers, with such force they erupted between his shoulder blades. The other bladed hand swiped across his neck, nearly separating his head from his shoulders. He yanked his extremities from the officer's body, and it slumped against the table.

Deep within the human molt that Wesley had become, there was welling guilt in his core. He had only wanted to resist—to defend himself justly—but his evolving appendages were too strong, too efficient. Feeling like a passenger behind his own eyes, he could only watch the ruthless evisceration.

The itching returned tenfold, this time in his face, a sensation of thousands of ants crawling behind his eyes. He scratched at it awkwardly with his permanently bent arms, raking at it with the rough spines. Wesley's vision blurred as his eyeballs swelled, inflated like bloodshot balloons in an almost comical manner. Together they popped with a hissing noise, rupturing like swollen cysts. What emerged from the ruined pupils was an expanded pair of compound eyes, glossy and red, reflecting the overhead fluorescence.

He was overcome with the newfound sensation of sight, seeing everything from every angle like some series of interconnected monitors. It was an apex sense of clarity; even the details had details, down to the microscopic level. He scanned the room, taking in every feature of the office with robotic precision. After several seconds, he craned his head behind him, where Dr. Sobieski was still cowering in the corner.

When Wesley finally walked, it was awkward but quick, as if spines were coming out of the bottoms of his feet, digging in for traction. He appeared in front of the elderly doctor in a blur. His calves bent backwards with every stride and worked like bony pistons. They seemed thinner and more agile compared to the growing bulk of his upper body. Walking on the pads of his feet, he felt like he could launch himself into the ceiling if he wanted to. Sobieski was sobbing now, pleading for mercy. Saying things like "I won't tell anyone" and "I didn't mean for this to happen". Bullshit lies—the ramblings of a scared, cornered animal.

"What's... *REEEEEE*—," Wesley's voice crackled with an ear-splitting shriek, but he fought to continue speaking, using what remained of his fleeting voice, "happening to me *DOOOOOOOC?*" Each screech produced a stringy salivation that drizzled from his chittering mouth. His voice was barely his own, merely a whisper of Wesley Porter. Even as he spoke it, it continued to sprout additional teeth, growing until his jaw broke free from his face

"I-I-I don't know! I've never seen something like this," He was hyperventilating, gasping and blubbering, but Wesley waited for him to continue. He towered over the old man, his crooked frame casting a spine-chilling shadow: a gurgling hiss transmitted passively while he waited, the sound of a thousand crickets singing in unison.

"I can't explain it. I don't know what's in you, son." He spoke fast and out of breath, "It could've been the radiation from the imaging, but I don't know. I almost didn't see it at first, but—" He stammered and began to weep again as Wesley was reaching out for him. The doctor surrendered and covered his face with both hands, sucking in breath and pushing it out as he wailed. Wesley's scythe-like arm was only inches away from his gullet, the protracted fingers twitching, almost touching him. The doctor whimpered and looked away, burying his face in his hands. Wesley's fingers snatched up the clipboard and held it in front of him so his large eyes could read it. The abdominal arms shot up, and cycled through the pages and film sheets with his miniature hands.

Wesley saw it now. He flipped through the pictures in order, seeing what had alarmed the doctor in the first place. In the first film, you saw nothing, just a normal skeleton. Then, little by little, a new bone structure was fusing around his, coiling around like barbed wire. It was paper-thin at first, but by the last image, they were growing, *bulking*. Feelers had spawned everywhere, intersecting and *weaving* into his insides. Wesley didn't know what it was, and it didn't matter. The irreversible damage was already done. The little stomach hands twisted the clipboard in frustration until it snapped in two.

Wesley turned to leave, but paused when he saw a hideous reflection in the mirror above the sink. He flinched at the sight of it, even though he knew it was him. His skin was stretched across a repulsive frame, limbs and shoulders of hardened carapace, decorated in strips of flesh like a gory Christmas tree. What was left of his face was worn like a mask, hiding the insect-like nightmare beneath his expired identity. As he stared at the reflection, antennae sprouted from his forehead, and twin trickles of blood made his massive eyes look like they were weeping. It matched the way he felt on the inside. He was a *monster*. The sadness haunted him over what he had done, but the officers had left him no choice.

Throwing his head back, he let out a supersonic cry, the terrible song vibrating everything in the room. The mirror above the sink shattered, raining pieces all over the counter and into the sink's drain. He ran from the room, shouldering through the door so hard it was ripped from its hinges. Pictures and posters were torn from the walls in his shambled run, awkward but purposeful steps raking the carpet beneath his feet. His legs carried him on autopilot as he weaved through the hall, escaping the chaos as fast as he could.

There was nobody to stop him along the way. The office was now a ghostly crypt, and Wesley moved through the halls like an apparition himself. When he came to the waiting room, his heart—what was left of it—ached, and there was a lump in his raw, sinewy throat.

The Lion King movie was over, the faint glow of the credits painting the room as they rolled endlessly down the screen. Where did he go from here? How did he come back from this?

Not knowing what to do, Wesley looked up at the ceiling of the waiting room and tried to think. The tubes of his brain felt like engorged maggots, squirming and packed tight within the shell of his new skull. His thoughts seemed to scream from them all at once, a shrill chorus of whines that drove him mad. Amidst the chaos and noise, there was a moment of comfort, a nanosecond of silence in his crowded mind.

There were one hundred fourteen tiles.

Wesley hissed and left the waiting room, ignoring the exit door's handle completely. Glass fractured and metal warped as it was forced out of his path. His all-seeing eyes scanned the parking lot, just in time to see a car pulling away. Tires spun in the gravel as it sped off. It must have been Cindy, running for her life. He didn't blame her.

The monster was outside now, tasting the sweet night air through its slit nostrils and its blender of a mouth. It took in every detail in its environment, from the shining stars to the worms in the earth. The antennae on its head twitched, and it picked up the siren of an inbound ambulance, two miles into the pitch-black horizon. It was time to leave this place.

It could hear something else, some unknown frequency that carried on the wind. Even without a visible trail, he could track the sensation, and it echoed with such significance that the monster knew where it had to go. As it disappeared into the trees, the shreds of its humanity faded away until there was nothing left but a tortured scream on the wind.

SKYLIGHTS

Jake was entranced by the scent of strawberry perfume. At this point in time, it was all that mattered to him. Every obsessive thought of school and scholarships was lost to him now, fading away against the weight of the magical scent.

The inside of his pickup cab was starting to fog, just like it did in the movies. Before now, he wasn't sure if it was a thing that really happened, but he knew now that it did. The *Def Leppard* playing softly on the radio seemed to set the mood right, making it feel like a fantasy. The beautiful blonde sharing the cab with him had scooted closer, leaning into him even. He could tell she was a little nervous, or at least he thought she was. Jake tried to act cool—to disguise the fact that his heart was beating a mile a minute, and his hands wanted to shake. But the perfume was getting stronger, almost intoxicating. He made a calculated move to reach out and pull her in closer, and to his relief, she scooted with it.

Jake kept one arm around her back and let his other hand fall on her waist. Her sundress was soft and thinner than he expected, and with his thumb, he could feel the firmness of her lean stomach, the unmistakable waistband of her underwear. He expected her to pull back or drift away, but she didn't. Instead, her hands found their way into his Letterman's jacket, onto his broad chest. He couldn't believe it was happening.

Stephanie Elizabeth was the girl's name, and she just so happened to be the girl of his dreams.

Jake and Stephanie both attended the same school in Dyer Falls, a small midwestern town known for its beautiful sights, competitive high-school sports, and—as of late—uncanny disappearances. It was a tight-knit community, enclosed by a mixture of farmland and dense forestation, wedged between a large city and the quiet neighboring town of New Sanctum.

Jake was a reserved student with few friends, aside from his peers on the football team. Usually timid and quiet despite his size, he wasn't the star player, and he wasn't popular with the girls. The only thing he ever thought he had going for him was his passion for weight lifting and his skill as a center-lineman for the Dyer Falls' Warlords. And like a Warlord, Jake was six-foot-five, and two-hundred-and seventy pounds of muscle.

Stephanie was a straight-A student and a track star. She was the fastest runner the school had to offer, and spent most of her time either putting miles under her belt or focusing on her schoolwork. Just like Jake, they were both seniors with promising futures. She was wanted by the popular crowd but avoided it for the most part, usually trying to distance herself from the drama that was always brewing at school. As far as Jake was concerned, she was *eons* out of his league.

Jake's pickup was parked at the top of Farmer's Point—one of the highest and most iconic spots in town. It was an alluring place that began with a winding, beaten path that led to a cliff on one side of town, offering an overlook that displayed miles of farmland, stretching all the way down the highway to the big city. The view was absolute magic, and with the way the city lights reflected off the sky, it would cast a glow over the hundreds of rows of corn below. It was well known by the high school students as "The Make-Out

Point", and at this moment, Jake and Stephanie were doing just that.

They spent minutes kissing, the only words spoken being on the radio. They seemed to move closer and closer, like some invisible gravitational tether was at work between them. He ran his calloused hands over her soft athletic body, slowly and gently. Stephanie explored his bulging chest, her fingers coaxing under his jacket and going over his shoulders, as far as her hands would fit. She was sitting right next to him now, as close as she could be without mushing him against the door; not that he would mind. Eventually, after what seemed like an eternity of contemplation, Jake's hand began to ascend, up her stomach, over the outline of her defined abdomen, briefly resting under her breast where he could feel the ever so slight framework of her rib cage.

Jake moved hesitantly, afraid of overstepping. Although he knew very little about her aside from her obvious hobbies, Jake cared for her and didn't want to come on too strong.

But now *Steelheart* was on the radio, and everything felt so *right.* Jake could only hope he wouldn't ruin things for himself.

As their lips met, he found himself opening his eyes so he could see her, to take in her face, her long hair. Every other time he had seen it, it was tied up in a ponytail. All those times, secretly admiring her from the scrimmage line, while the track team practiced on hot summer days. He took in all her features; her eyebrows, her cheeks, even her closed eyes. Everything he found so perfect from a distance was even better up close.

Jake was so lost in the moment that he didn't realize Stephanie was slowly sliding off his jacket. He paused, then assisted her by withdrawing his arms so he could worm them out of their sleeves. They briefly broke contact so Jake could toss his jacket on the dash, and Stephanie giggled. Jake pulled her back in close, running one hand through her hair while the other rested on her crossed legs. Her skin was warm to the touch, and only seemed to get warmer as he ran his hand slowly up to the top of her thigh, then slipped under the skirt of her dress. The kisses grew more intense, and Jake took that as a sign that he was doing all right.

Stephanie's arms draped around his neck while his hands moved. There wasn't a lot of room in the cab due to his size, but it only made them closer. The perfume continued to seduce him, a whisper of lust that entangled him with her. He ran his hand over her underwear, her lips curling into a smile as they kissed. His fingers graced her stomach slightly, and he felt her suck in a breath, which guided his hand to the top of her abs to the wire mesh of her bra. Feeling how defined her body was, he could only imagine how good it would look.

To his surprise, Stephanie stirred and pulled away. Jake's heart sank, and he felt a sudden shame that he had pushed too far. Before he could apologize, Stephanie uncrossed her legs and reached one over him to straddle his lap. Jake watched in disbelief. For a moment, they awkwardly readjusted to get situated, an endeavor that led Jake to adjust the steering wheel so she could fit. Once seated, Stephanie's hands found his chest again, and he felt her working her hips.

The desirable heat was almost too much for Jake. Now that it was grinding his erection against his leg, the sheer weight of the arousal was overwhelming. Jake didn't know how far she wanted to go, and his thoughts started to race. *Should he be more forward? He had a condom. Would getting it out be too much? Would she ask for it?* This was every boy's dream, but seeing it playing out in front of you was something different entirely. With Stephanie in his truck, parked out at Farmer's Point—it was what everyone joked about.

He couldn't help but feel lucky. She was here for *him*. Not the star quarterback, or the most popular guy. Somehow, he had done something right to earn it. He wanted to make sure he didn't fuck it up.

They pulled away briefly to catch their breath, both of them huffing as they stared into each other's eyes. Jake smiled, and so did she, and she bit her bottom lip as his hands traced the back of her thighs and grabbed her ass. It was just as firm as he imagined and nothing short of perfection. Stephanie leaned into him, grabbing fistfuls of his t-shirt as she pulled him into a very passionate kiss. Despite the cartwheels his mind was doing, Jake started to feel distracted, like something was nagging at him.

The music on the radio seemed louder than before.

He thought it was just in his head, or maybe they had nudged the volume dial somehow. He tried to ignore it and pulled her in for a tighter embrace. But as he felt her legs grind again, he could've *sworn* it was getting louder still.

Stephanie leaned back with a devious look in her eyes. She continued to stare into him as she blushed, her perfect lips curling into the perfect smile he had always wanted to see. Even as she slid down the straps of her dress, he felt drawn to the smile, like he was melting under it.

The radio continued to rise. The dash vibrated, and over the chorus of the sound, bursts of static started coming through. The two were more focused on each other, lost in their moment of passion. She looked like a goddess, the way her hair cascaded over her shoulders, her body flawless like an angel's. The static continued, cutting through more of the music, warping the vocals of the lead singer into a bizarre cry.

Jake was overwhelmed with emotions by the girl in front of him, so intense and overpowering, and he needed to speak to her. He didn't care about the repercussions; his heart couldn't take the wait any longer.

"Stephanie—" he called, trying to overthrow the mutating radio sounds.

She stopped for a moment and winced at the radio for a moment, before leaning in to hear him, mouthing the words "what".

"I think—I just wanted to tell you," he stammered, feeling suddenly nervous, "I think I love y—"

The radio screamed. An explosion of light followed, so blinding that it consumed the entirety of the truck's cab in an immediate blast. Jake and Stephanie jumped and shielded their eyes, but it was just too much—too strong to be blocked, no matter how hard they tried. The truck shifted so hard the vibrations shook their teeth and bones, and the only thing they could do was be crushed under the weight of the light and sound. Jake could barely see her screaming, and he pulled her close to protect her from the insanity, even though he didn't know if he could.

With the crushing sound, it was nearly impossible to even think. Everything shook so fast, Jake thought his brain would scramble and explode. The surging pressure built behind his eyes, nose, and ears. He feared his last living moments with his dream girl would end with his brain matter bursting from his skull, covering her in the very essence of his existence. It was sickening; he would give anything to have it end any other way. But Jake could only watch as the madness consumed them, cradling Stephanie to his chest with everything he had left.

The pickup bucked wildly to one side, tossing them to the opposite end of the cab. The impact knocked him harder than any tackle he had ever received. He couldn't feel any pain, but the pressure was bullying, assaulting them on a level foreign to this reality. The suppressing sound blocked all feeling of collision, but Jake held on, squeezing his eyes shut as the radio screamed with wild static. The momentum countered, and the truck shifted again. This time, the tires didn't grind into the dirt.

Defying gravity and logic, the truck was air-borne.

Jake opened his eyes to see cracks forming in the windshield. Time moved more slowly, crawling at a pace that made the light and sound grueling. He watched the cracks spread slowly, like a spider's web weaving before his eyes. As he struggled to comprehend what was happening, the glass detonated, a soundless explosion that dispersed thousands of fragments that tumbled towards him. The horrible bloom of shrapnel washed over them like a crashing wave.

He felt nothing from the impact, his body voiding every-thing under the immense *weight* of the light. He looked down at

Stephanie, her hair perpetually flowing in the madness, her face buried in his chest. As his vision began to flicker, the only thing gnawing at his brain was the regret of his own actions, knowing deep down that her fate was now sealed because of him.

After all the wonder and kindled love that had sparked moments ago, he wished he had never brought her there.

* * *

Darkness enveloped all. Jake flickered in and out of consciousness, only aware of his body's inability to scream. His body and mind felt fragmented, each individual scattered piece warped like torn gelatin. The sickening momentum made him feel as if he was going a million miles an hour and nowhere at all. A toxic bile felt chambered in his throat, and he wanted badly to purge, but he lacked the mental connection to contract his abdominal muscles. When it felt like the pieces of his being collected together, it hit with the sensation of being launched by a catapult by his ankles, only to be ripped around into a loop on repeat. Through the chaotic punishment, he thought only of Stephanie and hoped she was spared from such an act of cruelty.

Ringing- a frequency so piercing it began to wither away the sensation of spinning. The infinite void was shifting, changing, like a slideshow that cycled the hues until black faded to gray, and gray faded to white. Through burning eyes, he watched it change, each brighter shade stinging like he'd never seen light before. It was brilliant in its own nauseating way, like being pulled from a void. By the time the propulsion ceased, he was unaware of how much time had passed—only able to process that he had *stopped.*

One by one, his senses returned. His vision slowly gathered, like shaking stills sliding back into place. What was once black and white morphed into vibrant shades of red, yellow, and blue. It was as if his eyes were recalibrating. The primary colors melted into their secondaries, and the field of view before him started to make sense.

It was then that he realized he was lying face-down, in a room that was completely white.

The floor was cool against his skin. He felt the trickle of sweat on his brow, and the drying trails of what he assumed had been tears. His brain felt scrambled. His eyes felt like they would burst from their sockets. As the feeling of pain returned to him, a glimmer of a memory did as well. He tried to concentrate. In his freshly blended consciousness, his brain and his eyes connected the dots in unison. Details registered simultaneously, colors, shapes, movement and *fear*.

White. Pink. Purple. Black.

The truck. The cornfield. *The light.*

Stephanie.

Ahead, a glimmer of black and pink took shape, standing out amongst the stark white. What was once a shivering blur was now taking form, and his eyes could finally translate what was in front of him. Pink was the color of Stephanie's dress. He could see it now, still hanging slack on her hips. She didn't have time to pull it back up. She shuffled away but not without help, and as he watched, he could hear the squeak of her shoes against the floor. Upright and moving—but not of her own accord. He could see the figure then. Thin, dark, and blurry. Like a living shadow. It was taking her away.

Jake tried to move, keeping his gaze on the dress. He commanded effort into his limbs, but they didn't feel connected to his body. It felt as if his muscles had been simply shut off. His eyes darted around in a panic, looking for something, *anything* to help him. They were in some kind of room—he couldn't tell how big exactly. The walls were solid white, but looked so strange he didn't know if they were walls at all. Bulbless fluorescent against what looked like plexiglass. The floor was the same, but there seemed to be something *playing* underneath its tile-like design. It was unlike anything he had ever seen.

Animated, scribbled lines. They seemed to respond to the ringing that still resonated in his head, like the jagged movement you would see on a heart monitor. But there were thousands of them. He followed their trail—and watched the animated scrawls echo in front of him. With every step, they resonated around the figure that was taking Stephanie away.

A confused anger grew within him as he watched the figure that held her, a being that looked to be more shadow than human. He tried to focus on the details of the individual, but after enough observation, all he could feel was fear. The being had no features. No clothing or hair, not even skin. Just a clear layer containing an inky swirling mass that reminded him of oil. It was like a slender water balloon filled with pure black liquid. But there was no mistaking the human shape. And the way it moved, just like a human, except it was simply not right, almost like it was twitching in place, but moving nonetheless. It had Stephanie's arm slung over its shoulder, with its own arm wrapped around her waist as it ushered her away. She appeared unconscious, her limbs dangling helplessly.

Hugging the right side of the room were two tables about waist height. Jake couldn't see what was on them, but they were very pristine, the kind of things you would see in a hospital. Positioned next to them were two taller and longer tables, each holding something that looked like a large black bag. Both were unzipped and flayed open, revealing nothing inside.

Jake stared at the bags on the tables, a single bead of sweat running along his brow and dripped to the floor below. The jagged lines stirred like a group of fish, swaying side to side in unison. A nagging feeling picked at his brain, something that had been standing on the sidelines as the events had unfolded. Jake had seen enough movies as a kid to put two and two together, but he just didn't want to believe it. The truck. The lights. The intense sound and now this mysterious figure. Jake looked at the bags, innocently splayed across the gurneys. One of them was a little shorter than the other. It was narrower too, much narrower. Even now, the shadowy being was working his way towards the tables, moving slowly to accommodate Stephanie's dead weight.

One for me. One for her.

He wanted to scream until his lungs gave out, but the breath wasn't there. Completely immobile. Helpless. Jake watched as it took her away, who had shared the cab in his truck just moments ago. The one he had watched for so long, passing him in the halls so many times, before he mustered the courage to speak to her. And the feelings she must have had to do the things that she did and show the things that she showed. It had to mean something. It had to. She could've been with someone else, but she wasn't. She chose him out of everyone around her. He knew he had just really met her, and despite how fast they moved, he knew nothing about her. But he wanted to. It didn't matter what was about to happen. He knew she had felt something in the truck at Farmer's Point. Even if it was just a glimmer, it was good enough for him. No matter how small, it was something worth fighting for. He had to try.

No. You have to move. NOW.

With every ounce of his being, Jake tried to regain control of his comatose body. There was nothing at first. He could feel the restraints within himself, but he fought against them, trying as hard as he could to break the invisible chains that held him in place. He tried to scream, to call out to her. He wanted her to know he was here and that she wasn't alone. His lips twitched, and he tried to speak. However, all he could make was a whisper. He pushed without end, fueling the fire within himself. The flames burned, and his body ached, but he kept pushing. He pushed until it felt like his eyes would burst from their sockets.

"Stephanie!"

His voice was hoarse and dry, but it echoed in the stillness of the room. The shadow man stopped. The lines on the floor jumped into a frenzy, almost as if they were running in fright. They bounced across the floor and huddled around the shadow man, making his inky body vibrate in response. A distinct whining noise filled the room, a high-pitched hum that broadcast from the alien's direction. He could see Stephanie stir softly, as if she was tossing in her sleep. Stephanie's kidnapper continued to vibrate and twitch faster until it jerked suddenly, its head snapping back to look at Jake. Its face was a solid mass without expression. There was no mouth or nose—the only recognizable thing was two swirling pools that served as eyes. The humming grew louder and more distorted, into a rapid succession of static whines that seemed like some sort of communication. Jake yelled for Stephanie again, his voice growing a little louder.

With an uncanny movement, the shadow being raised an arm and pointed a single elongated finger at Jake. He stared into the black swirls—they reminded him of the eye that forms in a hurricane. Stephanie stirred again, but this time she opened her eyes. He could see the unquestionable fear on her face as she took in the room, the surroundings, and inevitably the shadow being. She looked like she wanted to scream, but her body looked like it was trying to throw up. She didn't have the strength to fight. When she saw him struggling on the floor, tears welled in her eyes. She held her gaze and mouthed a single word: "Jake".

The anger burned fiercely now, and Jake could finally feel himself moving. It was excruciating and slow, but he was getting back control. It required extreme effort, but the movement gave him hope, and he slid both arms across the floor until they were held out in front of him. Shaking fingers curled into fists. He pressed them against the floor, using them to push himself up. The sedation felt as if it was actively fatiguing him, but he kept pushing. Jake forced his neck up to look at them and cried out to Stephanie again. The shadow responded with a loud hum, and Jake felt two crushing weights slam onto his back.

The humming painfully pierced his ears. A set of black hands grabbed his forearms, while another set dug into his shoulders. He could see the abnormally long fingers reaching so far that they went past his collarbones. Two shadows were restraining him now; had they been there the whole time? Their eyes were the same menacing swirl, and their skin shimmered in the same manner. They spoke inaudibly to the one holding Stephanie, and he felt their speech raise the hair on the back of his neck like static.

Jake resisted with all his might, trying to gain any ground he could. Their fingers squeezed his shoulders and arms. The pain startled him, but he fought against them, even as he felt their digits break his skin and dig into the muscle. He was dizzy, and the ringing only made it worse. The glaring light of the floor made him nauseous.

Stephanie tried calling out to him, her shattered voice cracking in and out as she screamed. Her legs stiffened, and the shadow being adjusted his grip tighter. It kept its ominous gaze on Jake, even as it held her struggling weight. Her shoes squeaked on the surface of the floor, and her hanging dress fluttered softly. Jake continued to push against his aggressors, feeling the warmth of blood run down the center of his chest as they dug their fingers in more. He watched the being ahead, just a few feet away from those open bags. She was trying to resist them as well.

She continued to cry out, tears streaming down both cheeks. Her bronze hair swayed as she squirmed, the stray hairs brushing against the being's arm, vibrating as if they were being repelled. Stephanie's voice broke through, and she called out to Jake. The only thing she could move were her fingers, and she pointed them at him, almost as if the gravitational tether had followed them here.

The shadow man ahead flinched at her cry, and the crackling static burst into a growl. It sounded like a demon trying to pry its way out of a radio. The futuristic floor beneath them danced like a live sketch, wiggling violently like tentacles from the being's feet. The entities restraining Jake applied more pressure, and Stephanie shouted for him again, her voice coming through clearer each time she used it. This time, the being grabbed her by the throat. Its long fingers wrapped around her neck completely, squeezing until it cut off all sound. Stephanie tried to choke and cough, but could only hang there, her mouth agape as the blood collected in her face.

Something inside Jake snapped, like a locked door being ripped apart, hinges and all. A deep roar escaped from Jake's throat, and he thrashed uncontrollably. His humanoid restraints pushed back to contain him, their static speech attacked his ears, but he ignored it. His vision blurred as the fire within him exploded. He felt as if a hammer was crashing down, striking the red-hot irons that were his joints. With a battle cry, his right hand shot out and snatched the thin wrist that was holding down his left arm. The being he grabbed flinched and let go, freeing his other hand as it tried to regain its composure. With his hands now free, Jake grabbed onto the elbow as well and broke the arm backwards. It sounded like a board snapping in half.

An unnatural squealing wailed from the injured being, and it fell to the floor, clutching the limp arm that flailed about. The computerized floor tentacles went crazy, followed by an infuriated growl from the entity that was choking Stephanie. On his knees now, Jake felt the other captor holding him down slam into his back, wrapping both arms around his large upper body in a last effort to maintain control. Jake dug his boots into the floor for traction and pushed, launching the two of them forward and on top of the writhing being in front of them. With his arm bent, he shoved his elbow down upon the crippled alien's neck, using the combined weight of him and his mount to press it all the way to the floor. Jake watched as its head bulged, the dark mass inside swirling furiously until the eyes were pulled into the vortex.

The being holding Stephanie released a pulsating scream as the bulging head burst from the top, spewing putrid ink across the screen of the floor. The contrast of it was sobering, like watching a splatter of black paint on an LED canvas. The flat-lines raced away from the liquid, all the while maintaining contact between the two remaining shadows. Jake thrashed with his jockey, working his way back to his feet. His legs worked like a hydraulic machine. With one defeated, Jake could feel the other growing considerably weaker.

Jake worked his way to his feet. His legs shook at first, but they improved as he used the muscles, the pumping blood pushing through the sedation. The shadow tried unsuccessfully to subdue him, and he wrestled with the limbs as they tried to choke them out. When he found his footing, he lifted the shadow off the ground and steered his weight to the left, slamming the alien riding him into the wall. It was hard, like bulletproof glass. The collision loosened its grip immediately, and Jake took the opportunity to wrestle it in front of him. The alien's shadowy arms grabbed at his face as he launched his meaty fist into its gut. His punch blasted through the alien's stomach like a piston, soaring into the dark substance within until it broke through the wiry linkage that served as its spine. The being's grasping arms went slack, and Jake tossed it aside, watching it collapse helplessly with spurts of the black oily substance it contained. Jake could hear the growing intensity of the remaining entity, but he didn't care. After two bounding steps, he stomped the defeated alien, his size thirteen rattling the screen-like floor through the gooey carcass. The black liquid splashed his face and soaked into his shirt, darkening the fabric that stretched across his broad torso.

His stained fists were clenched so tightly that they were shaking. The digits ached as he made them into solid rocks. Jake felt overwhelming emotions: fear, desperation, and anger. He felt tears working through the black splatter.

Beneath the lifeless body he was standing on, the dancing lines in the floor loosened and detached. Jake watched not only as they left the body below, but the one whose arm he had broken as well. They wiggled and swayed together as they withdrew, all of them returning to the same focal point. They danced around the feet of the last entity, rotating like an electric sun.

There was something about the way the last one stood. It was more imposing than the others, its swirling eyes getting larger in the void of its face. It pointed at Jake in anger, its other hand coiling tighter around Stephanie's throat. It held her a foot off the ground, her face showing a light shade of blue. The look on her face made Jake yell in anger, but what he said, he didn't really know. He was seeing red now, gritting his teeth so hard they hurt.

The lead entity responded with its own crackling scream, as if to challenge him. The pool that served as its mouth grumbled, and it almost looked to be smiling.

Jake kicked the body that clung to his foot, sending it sprawling as he brought his foot forward into a harder stomp than before. The dark matter violently shook from his boot as his soles gripped the glass. Jake dug deep, letting his giant thighs propel him into a full sprint. Despite his size, he gained speed from raw power, lumbering ahead like a freight train. The entity pulled back his free arm as Stephanie kicked weakly, like it was going to underhand a baseball. In a split second, Jake crossed the distance and dove, aiming to tackle it. As the entity threw its arm up in a curling motion, another shriek poured from its gargling mouth. Jake could only watch in slow motion as a sickening fission ensued.

More dark mass protruded from the entity, emerging from the top of his wrist, all the way down his midsection. Another shadow being split off from it, quickly birthed through a mess of darkness and strands of ink.

The clone raised its hands in defense as Jake crashed into it, slamming it in the chest with a perfect shoulder takedown. The lead entity side-stepped to evade, the oily strands growing thin and snapping as Jake crushed the summoned clone against the floor. By the time they slid to a halt, Jake was already mauling it, pummeling its face with hammer-like fists.

In seconds, the clone was a lifeless corpse, its head reduced to nothing but a splattered mess. Jake rose again, his chest huffing as he turned to face the entity again. This time it craned its head towards Jake, the swirling pool eyes compressing and inclining towards its rumbling mouth. It looked frustrated now, furious even. It stole a look at the destroyed clone, then returned to look at Jake. The shrieking continued to rise, and the smile stretched into a gnashing maw of liquid teeth. Thousands of dancing lines at his feet sprouted and spun so fast they seemed to smear together.

Without another sound, the lead entity tossed Stephanie aside. She fell into one of the smaller tables, causing a hail of bouncing metal instruments that clattered across the now-stained computer floor. Her limbs shook as she curled her body on the floor, and with a loud suck of air, she coughed as she could breathe again.

Before Jake could make a move, the entity was already closing in, snarling like a rabid dog. Jake went to throw a punch, but he was too late. In one quick motion, the entity raised its arms in the air, and he watched as they split into bulging tentacles. It brought them down like cracking whips, slashing at Jake's shoulders, face, and chest. It was much stronger and faster than the others, and before Jake knew it, the tentacles were coiling around him with crushing force. He felt his muscles squeeze and twist as the feelers wrapped, like they were wringing out a towel.

Jake grit his teeth as he tried to hold his footing, straining his back and shoulders as he struggled against the snaking arms. The entity lifted him off the ground, the morphing limbs winding tighter as it dangled him like a plaything. It held Jake in front of his face and screamed, its shadowy mouth getting more twisted the louder it got. The coils squeezed and squeezed, and the crippling pain was starting to break through Jake's rage. He felt one of his shoulders on the brink of dislocation, a feeling of internal tearing that screamed throughout his body. Jake groaned through clenched teeth, and he felt the feelers wrap around his throat and strangle him. The blood collected in his face, and he felt as if his eyes would burst from his skull.

An excited cry emitted from the shadowy beast, tossing Jake from one side to another as he writhed in anguish. It viciously slammed him down, and the floor shook, the lines beneath scattered on the impact. He tucked his chin so his head wouldn't bounce, just like he would brace himself on the football field. It slammed him again to wear him down, but Jake held in, his legs kicking as the tendrils tried to consume him. Jake pulled whatever strength he had left and waved his arms outward, and curled them around to wrestle the tentacle arms. He grabbed handfuls of the spongy tentacles and yanked it towards him, lashing out his leg as hard as he could. His boot buried square into the entity's face as he kicked it, temporarily putting an end to the blaring static.

An electrical shockwave blasted across the futuristic floor, sending the jagged lines into a brief disarray. The coiling arms went slack but did not let go, letting Jake free-fall back to the floor. The pressure on his shoulders withdrew, but not by much, and he took it as his only opening. He whipped his arms in a circular motion, gathering the tentacles around his wrists to get the best hold he possibly could. Just as the entity started to recover from the kick, Jake swung his arms together, gripping the black arms so hard he started to tear through the membrane. As the static started up again, Jake twisted hard, throwing both arms to toss the alien off its feet. The entity slammed into the wall with such force that it shook the room, rattling the lights above.

The lines on the floor dispersed once more, dancing away in a panic as the entity stumbled with gelatin legs. Jake felt the vibrations through his boots, the electrical change crawling across his skin. The tentacles went slack again. Jake watched it stagger, wanting it to just stop so this could be done. It hunched over as it recovered, the lines in the floor trying to find their way back into position. Jake drove his knee upward, and it met right below its chest. The weakened black body bucked wildly, the arms held on. The static fizzled and popped, the lines still struggling to come back to their master. Jake grunted and drove it home again, this time catching it right under the jaw. Its swirling head bobbed around, but still it maintained its hold. So Jake did it again. And again. And again.

Jake tore into the being without end. Knee after knee after knee until it felt like he was beating a training dummy. But still it held on, the same tight coils constricting with what seemed to be endless strength. He continued to lay into it, hitting it harder and harder until he could see the wiry linkage inside break into dozens of floating pieces. The torso was reduced to nothing but a softened husk, but it did not break, no matter how many times he struck it. His abs started to burn, and he was drenched in sweat.

The limp torso continued to flop on wobbling legs, all of its strength focused on the tentacle arms. In desperate frustration, Jake lashed out at the legs, breaking one to the side at an awkward angle. He stomped the knee of the other until it broke backward, leaving it nothing to stand on. But still the arms held unrelentingly. Jake just wanted it to stop. He wanted it to be over.

The beaten entity lay there limp, a lifeless body hanging from tangled limbs. Jake huffed for breath as the exhaustion took its toll. He was running out of steam, his hips and stomach sore from treating the being as a kick bag. His shoulders throbbed from the constriction, every joint crunching together from the abuse. He shook the alien, trying to find some sign of life so he could find a way to extinguish it. Its bobbing head lolled to one side and stayed there, letting Jake see its face. The oily face was blank; every previous movement had ceased to be a stagnant surface. The vessel of its head was tattered and filled with dents. The swirling eyes were gone. Feeling the rage fade, Jake stared into the black face with confusion. It was done.

The sounds of contorted leather echoed as Jake wrestled with the tentacles to remove them. The host was completely spent, but still the grip remained. He fought and fought to get it off, feeling his elbows ache tremendously as he overworked them. After several struggles, he stopped, standing there in the silence that now filled the room. The only sounds came from him as he tried to breathe; every vibration and hum he once heard had vanished. The ringing had disappeared from his ears, leaving him with nothing but utter silence. He looked around the room at the other defeated beings, still lying frozen in a pool of their own dark substance. He didn't understand. Why was this thing still holding on to him?

A deafening blast exploded through the room. The floor shook so intensely that Jake's feet slipped, unable to hold any traction at all. The vibrations were back tenfold, shaking everything so hard Jake couldn't see straight. The jagged lines on the floor reappeared and danced, thousands of them, *millions*. The lead entity was staring at him now, his swirling eyes taking up its entire face. As Jake looked into them, it made him think of death itself, two black holes sucking up everything around them. A distorted laugh of white noise cackled from it, so deep and powerful it pushed back Jake's hair and matted his face with every chuckle. The monster slammed into him, taking the wind from his lungs as it took him down.

The lead entity twisted and thrashed, throwing Jake's head repeatedly into the floor. He kicked his feet and turned his body in protest, but he was no match for the alien's newly evolved strength. He tried to grab at its broken legs with his boots, but they weren't legs anymore. They oozed and bled together, inky strands pulling it into a solid tail that was starting to snake around both of Jake's legs. He kicked to stay free, but the tail crushed his legs together.

The nightmarish evolution continued to laugh, even as an additional set of tentacles peeled out of his back. They stretched out like wings, splitting into dozens of feelers that cast a shadow on Jake. All he could do was watch as the monster towered above him. He tried to free himself, tried to bounce back, but there was no hope. He even bit into one of the coiled tentacles, but the entity only laughed when he spit out the oily fluid.

Crying like a mechanical banshee, the alien brought the wings down one at a time, pummeling Jake over and over again. The feelers whipped at him, splitting his brows and breaking his nose. Unable to defend himself, Jake watched as the masses rose and fell upon him, every consecutive blow blurring his vision as he started to slip out of consciousness. The entity slammed one wing down to hold him in place while the other melded into a boulder shape, rearing it back to finish him off. It swung like a wrecking ball, and as the tentacles buried Jake, he watched the incoming doom through a slit in the dark mass.

Jake felt the weight of utter defeat as the tentacles buried him. It wasn't sadness he felt but regret, wishing there were more he could do. His entire body was pummeled, but he didn't care. Blood bubbled from his mouth and seeped into his eyes, but it meant nothing. In his misery, he thought of Stephanie, and he thought that if there was one last thing he could do, he would tell her he was sorry. With a single eye, he looked to his right, near the tables where she had fallen. He looked for her perfect face, but she was nowhere to be found. Stephanie was gone.

A glint of light shone above, and he looked up, watching as a sharp piece of steel dug into one of the entity's eyes. Oily blood spewed down on him, splashing the twitching tentacles that were now starting to loosen around him. In the glow of the fluorescents, Jake watched as Stephanie shoved the scalpel-shaped instrument into the swirling mass, holding on to the tentacles to keep from falling. The nightmare writhed and screamed, but that only made her drive it further. She had one of her dress straps on now, half of her bra still exposed as she buried the scalpel with both hands. Jake felt the tension lift from his shoulder, several of the feelers pulling back to divert to his dream girl. He worked his hands free through the squirming layers and latched onto one, using it to pull himself ou t.

Working through the shadowy mass, he twisted the membrane with both hands until it tore apart. The entity howled and pulled back its wing and swung, this time hurtling it towards Stephanie. Jake dove from his inky prison, shielding her as he wrapped both thick arms around the incoming wing. The force slammed Jake and pushed him into Stephanie, knocking her off balance from the dark mass. The scalpel yanked free as she fell backward. Jake reached out and caught her by the arm. Briefly, their eyes met, and he saw a glimmer of hope, with the slightest curl of a smile. She nodded, and he knew he had to keep going. With a final battle cry, Jake swung her forward, and Stephanie stabbed into the monster once more.

Together they climbed the mountain of shadow, even as it continued to grow. The static shock tried to blast them away, but they didn't falter. The entity howled every time Stephanie drove the scalpel in, ripping and tearing through the membrane as she worked her way up. Stretching and pulsing, the nightmare loomed as it struggled with the two of them. The lines on the computer floor flashed faster, giving off a projection of strobe lights. The tentacles whipped and slashed at them through the lights, but they missed their marks. Stephanie swung one of her long legs and kicked at its midsection, her leg acting as a club. Jake dug both feet into the membrane and jumped skyward, bringing his fists together for a final devastating blow. The entity looked up at him, a single inky eye struggling to spin as the other bled profusely. As gravity pulled him back down, Jake slammed both fists on the remaining eye, watching it crumble away. Stephanie slashed across its neck with her weapon, parting the membrane that supported its crushed head. A tentacle wrapped around her leg, and she carved into it more
.

Down the mountain came, tilting backward like a falling tree. Together they rode it to the ground, Jake throwing blows and Stephanie stabbing as they descended. The lead entity hit the floor, its ruined head bouncing off the glass. Before it could make another noise, Jake buried his fist in its forehead, so hard he thought his knuckles would break against the oily glass. The head blew apart in a violent mess, its vague facial features reduced to nothing. Its shrinking torso twitched to stay alive, the thousands of floor lines scattering in panic with every oozing spurt, like the life force was fading away. Stephanie impaled the entity's throat, twisting the knife until it was nothing but a torn plastic bag. The lines on the floor emitted a pitiful whining noise, fluttering away one by one until there was barely any left. Jake sifted through the exploded head, finding something left to grab on to. Digging his fingers into what would be its jaw, Jake grabbed it and tore the head off.

Still holding the mutilated head, Jake stepped off the heap and rested his back against the wall, the severed head spewing into a sparkling monochrome mess. They both stood speechless, the huffs of their fatigue and the squelching of the deflating corpses acting as their applause for victory. Jake looked at the featureless balloon-like skull in his hands and squeezed it into mush, watching the black ooze bleed through his fingers before letting it go. When he heard the *plap* of it hitting the floor, he felt a sudden utter exhaustion, like all of his energy had been sucked away. Every muscle in his body felt torn and completely spent.

Through heavy, clouded eyes, he saw Stephanie approach him and heard the sharp sound of tearing fabric. She started blotting his eyes softly, and when he could see better, he saw she had ripped it from her dress. Even covered in dark matter, she looked beautiful as ever. She pressed the wad of cloth to his nose, trying to soak it up as it gushed. He winced against the jolt from the ruined cartilage. Stephanie tore another strip and used it to wipe his brow and what had collected around his eyes. While she tended to him, she glanced between him and the dead captors. Their devastated bodies looked like ink blots on the digital canvas. The lines were gone now, an eerie silence in their absence.

"Are you okay?" she asked, her voice shaken.

It was wonderful to just hear her voice after nothing but static for so long. Jake nodded, looking at the purple bruise that had formed across her throat. He reached for it, and she waved him off, embarrassed.

"It's alright. Just took me a moment to get my second wind, that's all," she chuckled, shaking her head, "It's stupid, really." She smiled, but there was a crack in it. He grabbed the hanging strap of her dress and pulled it back over her arm, working around the scalpel she was holding. His hands were shaking, the adrenaline fleeting the longer he stood still. Her lip quivered as she tried not to cry.

"It's okay," Jake said, his voice coarse and dry, "We made it. It's done." He caressed her cheek and wiped the tear away with his thumb, taking a couple of specks of ink with it. Stephanie rolled her eyes, but he could see the walls coming down. Holding the wad to his nose, he offered an arm weakly for a hug, and she nodded and embraced him.

"Where are we? How did we get here?" She asked, softly crying into his chest. Jake held her tight, looking at the madness around them. Now that the fighting was over and he could actually process their situation, the existential weight was crushing.

"I don't know." He felt his own tears now, and before he knew it they were weeping together.

"I want to go home," she whispered.

"I know. Me too. We'll figure it out," he said, and for a time they just stood there, rocking silently back and forth. Jake closed his eyes and enjoyed her embrace, the scent of strawberry perfume finding its way through the metallic staleness of the room they were in. He felt his kindled anger fade, and as their tears met an end. Stephanie sniffled and pulled away

"When we were in the truck, before this," she paused, wiping her eyes with the back of her hand, "You were trying to tell me something. I couldn't hear you very well, and then, well, all this-" She waved her hand at the crumpled dead, and the sight that spoke for itself, "-what were you going to tell me?"

They looked at each other for a moment, the invisible tether pulling them together. Jake reached for her and pulled her in, kissing her softly. She leaned into him, just as she had when they were in the truck. Jake let his hands rest on her hips, and she looked up at him with puffy eyes.

"I love you, Stephanie."

Stephanie buried her face into his chest and cried. Jake held her tight and kissed her forehead, running his hands up and down her back as he tried to comfort her. He looked at their surroundings, taking in everything now that it was quiet. All the bodies, sketchy instruments lying around, and that damned computer floor.

He didn't know how they were going to get home, and he tried not to think about it. One step at a time. That's all they could do. He leaned his head against hers, and he could still smell the strawberry perfume, wafting through the disgusting splatter that covered them both. As they rocked in place, he wished he could just stand here forever, holding her so he wouldn't have to worry about anything else.

"I love you too," Stephanie responded, her head on his chest. She wasn't crying anymore, but her eyes were still closed. Jake smiled, and it seemed to give his beaten body a surge of life. He just watched her, her hair a tangled mess, her make-up smeared down her cheeks.

Jake let his gaze drift to the computer floor, trailing off as they held each other. At the far end of the room, there was a window, behind where he was when he woke from the abduction. It stood out now, a cut-out square dead in the center.

Off in the distance was Earth, floating like an immaculate marble. It was so bright and distinct that it almost looked fake. Jake thought he was crying, but he couldn't really tell. They really were in space.

While he was mesmerized by the view, he suddenly looked away. He swore he saw one of the bodies twitch. There was nothing for a time, and he thought his eyes were playing tricks on him. Maybe he had a concussion—maybe even brain damage. But when he saw the liquid move, slowly rising from the exploded chest cavity of the one he had stomped to death, he knew that wasn't the case.

Jake felt the fear reignite within him as he watched the impossible unfold like a bad dream. A perfectly sculpted head emerged from the substance, staring with two swirling eyes. Jake blinked, hoping he was imagining it. A second followed suit, a pair of oily hands parting the ruptured head that served as its cocoon. This wasn't happening. It wasn't fair. They had won.

"Shit," Jake said, and Stephanie looked up at him to see what was wrong. He didn't want her to look, but when she followed his gaze, she gasped, watching in horror as the shadows emerged from their broken vessels.

The jagged lines beneath the floor returned, slithering like snakes. They rose one by one, their undamaged bodies emitting the same soft frequency as before. They stood and took a moment to admire their new, restored bodies before doing something that made their hearts sink. Jake and Stephanie watched as they twitched in place and *split*. Two became four, the oily strands snapping as the clones peeled into existence. They continued to multiply, stopping only for a second before splitting again. Eight. Sixteen. Their numbers grew rapidly, all of them tethering across the floor, connecting to the eviscerated leader that lay at their feet. The headless body was now sitting up, oily liquid still oozing from the stump above its shoulders. The tentacles meshed together into the original arms, and elbows and wrists snapped back into shape.

Jake moved away slowly, pulling Stephanie with him. He didn't go far, but he wanted to put some distance between them. The crowd of shadows watched silently, their heads following in unison.

Jake and Stephanie looked at each other, then back at the aliens, dozens of eyes swirling, watching them like cornered prey. They backed away more, but there was nowhere to go. Jake's hip nudged against the gurney with the larger black bag. He peered into the nothingness of the empty bag, knowing they intended to fill it with him. There was no way around it. They wouldn't stop until they got what they wanted. Jake took one more look at Stephanie, who was looking back. Her face told him she was thinking the same thing, coming to the same conclusion.

Ahead, the lead entity was on its feet, picking its ruined head off the floor. He held it in both hands, positioning it above the stump until it sucked back into place. Its head sealed and reflated, and it cracked its neck as the swirling eyes returned bigger than the other clones. It didn't look at Stephanie but at Jake, a deep laughter echoing as it mocked him.

Jake looked at the lead, then at the multiple other clones that now stood before them. They just watched him as the leader laughed, their emotionless faces remaining still as they twitched in place. With a deep breath, Jake stepped forward and stood in front of Stephanie, acting as a wall in front of her. He balled his hands again, and his sore knuckles cracked. Several of the clones turned their heads to one side as if intrigued. The leader only laughed louder, making him feel as small as he could. He decided it could laugh all it wanted.

With his head held high, Jake stood up to them, taking the time to make eye contact with each individual clone. They all stared back, some of them eager, others hesitant. The shadows intimidated him no longer. He knew he wouldn't be able to get through all of them, but he would get through some.

Jake felt a soft touch on his arm, and he looked to see Stephanie standing directly at his side. She was gathering her hair in both hands, tying it into a ponytail with the scalpel held in her teeth. She flicked her hair to let it settle, then held the scalpel ready. She gave him a nod and a smile that he couldn't help but return. They would stand against the odds together, knowing there was no way to win. It didn't matter if there were hundreds more; he had her by his side, and he knew they would fight back-to-back until they had nothing left.

Jake nodded solemnly and turned back to the group of clones, waiting for the shadows to descend upon them. After seconds, the whine of static wound up, and the flat-lines danced. The clone closest to them twitched and bolted forward, darting toward them with its fingers flattened like blades. Jake stepped forward and raised his fists, wondering how fast he could tear off its arm.

"ENOUGH!"

A booming voice echoed in the room, and the flat lines straightened, ceasing all movement. The clone ahead froze in place as if time had stopped, maintaining perfectly still mid-stride. The shadows looked at each other in confusion, their swirling eyes dissipating into a more passive demeanor. Together they twitched in unison. One by one, they drifted together, melting back into the host from which they spawned. Their numbers quickly diminished as they blinked together, disappearing until there were only two left standing in the crowd. After several twitches, the shadow went slack and began drifting, its head and arms hanging limply as it merged into the lead entity.

The leader snarled static and shook its head, appearing displeased with the turn of events. Stephanie looked at Jake, and he shrugged. Behind the growling leader, there was the sound of whooshing air, and the wall behind it began to shift. A portion of the wall separated from the rest and began to recede upward. A white mist floated in as a doorway materialized, opening onto another corridor that led to nothing but an abyss of darkness. The lead entity looked into the doorway, staring into the darkness as it continued to growl disappointedly. Jake watched as well, his hand feeling for Stephanie's. Their fingers interlocked as they waited for what was in store.

Through the wafting mist emerged another shadow man, one much taller than the others they had seen. The towering being floated in, garbed in a bright cloak that obscured everything but its neck and head. The cloak was made of static, like an untuned television. The collar of the cloak was flared out and wrapped around the back of its neck, protecting a wiry cage much like the spines of the beings he defeated. Its head was more enlarged, the top of its skull swollen into a bulbous crown. Tiny arcs of lighting traveled the surface of its head from the inside of its static cloak. The tall being floated to a stop just a few feet from the snarling entity, peering down at it with one massive singularity of an eye.

The taller being dwarfed its companion, almost bullying it with its giant swirling pupil.

The snarling entity muttered something inaudible and pointed to Jake and Stephanie, speaking to its master in a language that sounded like a broken radio. In response, the tall one just leaned in more, casting a shadow over the monster that almost beat Jake to death moments ago. The tension held for a moment, then ceased, resulting in the snarling entity bowing its head in obedience. With a single twitch, it turned back at Jake and growled, pointing one elongated finger before blinking out of existence. The shadow master straightened and looked at the two of them, the intimidating black eye just watching in silence. Stephanie squeezed Jake's hand, but she couldn't look away from the terror that stood before them.

"Marvelous. Absolutely marvelous," The shadowy master commented, floating closer as it spoke. It communicated in perfect English, but the static distorted its words. The voice was so powerful that it was almost as if Jake could hear it inside his head. The shadow master turned and floated towards the window, which seemed to grow in size to accommodate its height. With a steady hum, it looked out, its large swirling eye gazing upon the planet Earth and the darkness that surrounded it. The electrical arcs crawled over its head like elemental spiders.

"It's quite something.... isn't it? This object you call your home." The tall being turned away and floated towards them, his black eye getting more oppressive the closer it got. The jagged lines on the floor acted differently—they seemed to flick and billow around the entity like a jellyfish traveling through water. Jake looked up at it, feeling a single bead of sweat run down the side of his head.

"Tell me, do you know why you are here?" The alien asked, leaning its head in. Jake just stared at the black hole in its face. It was like looking at the complete absence of life. He shook his head, and he could feel Stephanie's hand trembling.

"I'll make this simple and to the point. Your home—a planet you call it, yes? Earth. Your planet is something much different than what you think it is. You live there. You call it your home. You inhabit it, and therefore you believe it belongs to you, don't you?"

The electricity arced from the cage, casting a glow over his brain-textured skull as they passed over it. Jake said nothing, just watching the shadow that towered over him.

"You see—your planet—it holds something more valuable than the water you drink or the air that you breathe. Something more than the organisms that you coexist with—even the resources your species has studied to develop. Every achievement your species builds, every sight you regard as a wonder, all holds no value, nothing at all. You see, your precious home has something that we do not, something that requires discovery. Something that must be obtained," The shadow master continued; its only form of gesture being the flowing of its static cloak. Jake swallowed, trying to imagine what was worth having that didn't consist of any kind of fuel or resource.

"The one thing your planet appears to be plentiful of, however, is space. You see, my kind, we do not require a singular place to exist. We do not need a home, because we exist out here, in the infinite plane that serves as your galaxy. We do not breathe air as you do, and we do not need to consume to survive. The only thing important to us is power, because we require it to run the very vessel you stand in. And without power, we are nothing, and to obtain this power, we must build. You see, we are only here for the sole purpose of annihilating your species, and to construct our reactors and pylons atop the rubble that would become of you."

Jake felt his stomach twist into knots, and the reality of it made him want to puke. It was much bigger than he thought, way bigger than he could imagine. At his side, he clenched his fist, wondering if he could stop it.

"*Now, now.* I know what you're thinking, and I would advise against it. You see, you would be vaporized before you could even lift that arm. And she would watch you fall into a pile of dust just moments before suffering the same fate. I am not a soldier like the ones you so bravely fought before me, but I'll have you know that I am more powerful than anything you will ever see in your entire existence. I have watched your world turn for more than a millennium, and not only yours, but thousands of others. But the reason I stand before you now in this room is not because of conflict, but because you've shown me something I haven't seen in a very, *very* long time."

Despite the fear and hatred Jake felt, he uncurled his fist and let it fall. He nodded, allowing the alien to continue. The tall being straightened, looking around the room before it spoke again.

"Getting to the point, you were to be harvested today. We brought you and your mate here to be dissected and analyzed, a routine precautionary action taken before the reconstruction of a new planet. It's something we've done many, many times before. It's nothing personal, as your kind would say. It's only the way of the galaxy you inhabit. You see, your eradication would be nothing more than what you would do to an insect under your boot. But you've shown me something today that was truly very impressive. Not just you, but the one who stands next to you now. When you arrived here, you knew the moment you opened your eyes that you would not survive. Even still, you fought against us to the very end, even when you knew you would fail. You displayed such animosity, such ruthlessness, and not just for your own safety, but for hers. And she did the same for you, stopping at nothing and standing together as one."

It paused for a moment, and the electricity crackled again.

"Something such as this makes me think; if only two of you are capable of such a display of unity, what would you be

capable of if there were more of you? It would be some-thing worth seeing, I imagine. But I will have you know, in the end, it still would not be enough to stop us." The shadow master paused again, as if giving them a second to ab-sorb what it had told them. Jake stared into the swirling vortex of its face, the darkness that circulated infinitely. He didn't need to see any evidence; he believed it was true.

"I understand this must be a lot to process for you, so I will bring this to a conclusion. The reason I am here in front of you now is not to inform you that your planet would be too difficult to obtain; it is to tell you it wouldn't be *convenient*. **After what you showed me in this room, I've decided that we should move on to another subject, something more easily obtained. What is it your kind says? Ah, that's it. You should be** *proud of yourselves*. **The things you've seen here today, the wounds you have sustained, remember them with everything that you are. Because if you were anything less than what you are today, there would have been a much different outcome. You have prolonged the future of your species."**

The tall one straightened and floated away, the lines on the floor gracefully fluttering behind it. It approached the flowing mist, making its way to the door of darkness.

"Wait—" Jake called out, hoping he wasn't making a mis-take. The tall being stopped and turned its head so the black hole could see. With the endless fog washing over its cloak, it waited, like it was curious what he had to say.

"What happens now? What do we do?" Jake asked, not entirely sure what to do next. Stephanie continued to hold his hand as she drew closer to him.

"We're sending you home. Exactly where we found you. Is there anything else you would like to ask before I depart?" The shadow master said, and Jake didn't know if the remark was out of annoyance or sincerity.

"How do we know? I mean, how do we know you're not just going to destroy us the moment we get back?" Jake asked. Even amidst their accomplishment, it made him realize how small he really was.

"Hmmmm. I guess you'll just have to take my word for it. But know this: when you return to your planet and resume your life, take a moment to look up at the sky that surrounds you. We will be watching."

***

Jake woke to the sound of Steelheart. It startled him so much his knees smacked the steering wheel, and his hand pressed the center of it. The blare of the horn echoed into the night and caused a stirring next to him. Stephanie was pulled out of her slumber, looking around wildly in the cab of the truck. She took in her surroundings, searching around her until her eyes rested on Jake.

"Oh my god. We're home," she said, and settled into the bench seat, hugging herself. She took a deep breath and closed her eyes, opening them again to make sure she was still there.

Jake looked outside, scouring the wild that surrounded them and saw nothing but trees and corn. His entire body was stiff, and he looked over himself, his clothes and shoes for some sort of proof of what had transpired. Every drop of blood had disappeared, and every black stain was gone from his clothes. Did it all really happen? Or was it all a dream?

"Yeah. We made it," he agreed, but he felt like there was something more to be said. But all the words were lost to him now, overwhelmed by the simple thought of being there, sitting in his truck.

"Did it... did it all really happen?" she asked, and her eyes welled up, not in sadness but in relief. She looked at her arms and her dress that was now perfectly clean. She looked at her shoes, holding out a long leg to take in all the details. Jake looked too, but saw nothing to support the conclusion they desired. He scanned her up and down, searching for some sort of clue. But when his eyes fell on her hair, he stopped. Her hair was pulled back, still bound in a ponytail.

"What? What is it?" She asked, and watched him scoot closer to her, an arm outstretched. Jake placed his hand on her hair, feeling the ponytail as he ran his fingers through it. Stephanie did the same, and when she felt the elastic loop bind, she froze, as if remembering when she had put it on. Her eyes locked with his, and she fell into his arms. She wrapped her arms around his back and rested a cheek on his chest, just like she did on the ship. Jake welcomed the embrace, wanting to do nothing more than sit here wi th her.

"It happened. It really did," she said, trailing off into silence as they both thought of the events they survived. The static shadows, the futuristic floor. It all really happened, and here they were, returned to the safety of the cab with the radio playing, just as it was before they took them.

"You told me you loved me..." Stephanie recalled, her words cutting through the music.

After a few seconds, Jake sat forward, making her pull back. She just looked at him, expecting something, wanting something. Jake reached the dashboard and grabbed his Letterman's jacket, which was still sitting where he had left it. He gave it a shake to flatten it out and placed it softly over Stephanie. The sheer size of the jacket made it perfect for a blanket, especially for someone her size. She grabbed it in both hands, pulling it to her chest as she tucked her legs in to snuggle beneath it.

"Yeah. I did," Jake admitted, giving her a soft smile. She smiled back and patted the empty space in the seat next to her.

Jake rolled his window down and scooted towards her, lying across the seat with his head on her lap. He poked his feet through the opening of the door and rested them on the windowsill. He felt exhausted, and as he sank into the comfort of the bench seat, he looked up at Stephanie. She caressed his short hair and ran her fingers along his scalp, the whole time maintaining that same perfect smile. He just gazed up at her, wanting the moment to last forever.

"Shit—" Stephanie said, and Jake started to sit up.

"What? What's wrong?" he asked, but Stephanie stopped him, her little hands pushing on his chest until he was returned to her lap.

"Nothing, it's nothing. It's just that I forgot I had a track meet tomorrow. After school," she said, and Jake laughed slightly, breathing a sigh of relief. He nestled back into her lap, using her legs as firm pillows.

"You want me to be there?" he asked, looking up at her. She smiled again, and he realized he would never get tired of seeing it.

"I would love that," she said and kissed his forehead.

Together they looked out the window, watching the city lights across the field of corn. It was beautiful, the way the light reflected off the crops, which seemed to beam up into the sky. The warm night air wafted through the trees and into the cab, reminding them of the sweetness of being home. They looked up at the stars, seeing the several glinting shapes in the sky, each of them unique and brilliant.

And amongst the millions of stars that covered their world, one of them blinked away, as if it was never even there.

I'M BEING MUGGED

The frosted shot glass was inviting. Wendell looked down at it like a marquis diamond, the unclouded liquid twinkling in the light on the polished bar counter. The bottle's essence made him think of melted glass, so clear and crystalline you could swear it was chilled water. The bartender watched him, observing, almost worrying if something was amiss. He guessed his name to be Leroy, since that was the name of the establishment, and he was the only one serving drinks. He even looked like a Leroy.

"Something wrong, friend? Unfortunately, even the stuff on the top shelf looks about the same when you pour it out," Leroy said, clearly hoping to ease whatever discomfort his new customer seemed to have.

"No, all is well," Wendell assured and grabbed the glass, feeling the icy condensation as he pinched it between his two fingers. "It's amazing how something so clear and beautiful," Wendell continued, raising the little glass as if he was peering through it, "could taste so foul."

He knocked it back, feeling the cold fire go down his throat and burn just the way he liked it. The liquor was a true wolf in sheep's clothing; an assassin garbed in the finest robes of true clarity. Vodka was his favorite, and if he had to guess, this was probably the three-hundredth bottle he had sampled from, or something close to it. It didn't matter if it was triple, quadruple, or quintuple distilled; it all tasted about the same, despite how "smooth" it was claimed to be.

"I'll have another!" declared Wendell, after he had completely absorbed the burn. Leroy appeared pleased and wasted no time obliging. Wendell watched the shooter fill, practically licking his lips in excitement. Leroy capped the bottle and set it on the bar. Wendell knocked it back faster than the previous one, and it went even smoother. Wendell gritted his teeth against the heat and smacked the top of the bar.

"Well, *goddamn!* I'll take it!" Wendell gave a hoot, heat flushing his cheeks. It would truly be a fine companion for the night. He pulled out his wallet, a bifold of thick maroon leather that was stamped with a cursive 'W'. He felt that if he needed something to carry so much of his hard-earned money, it would have to have his name on it.

Leroy was hesitant at first.

"Are you positive, sir? Surely you could find this same bottle at a better price at the liquor store down the block," he said, and his generosity took Wendell aback.

This was definitely a man who cared for his customers.

"Of course. I've always found something special about finding the right one at the source. Not to mention I'm very pleased with your... hospitality. I would be delighted to see you take the dime," Wendell said, already rifling through the bills in his wallet.

Leroy seemed to think it over for a moment before the smile crept upon his face.

"Would you like a bag?"

Wendell strolled out of the bar in that jolly way you do when you've pounded two shots back-to-back and they're starting to loosen you up. The night air was cool, and the breeze was welcoming. It was a nice evening for a stroll, even in the congested mess of a big city. There was hardly anybody out and barely a car in sight. The sight was pleasant to him, until he noticed the lack of yellow cabs.

He looked both ways down the vacant street, holding the ruffled paper bag in the crook of his arm. Wendell thought maybe he could wait it out, see if one would roll around the corner. As the impatient seconds passed, he considered calling one. That wouldn't take long, surely. His thoughts fluttered as he considered his options. The weather was just so *right,* and the recent consumption left him feeling fuzzy and warm. It wasn't long until the idea of waiting for a cab started to feel daunting.

I could just walk, he thought harmlessly. By the time the calculation of the cab fare popped into his head, the decision had already made itself.

Time was precious; time was money. And Wendell never spent that money unless it was absolutely necessary. Or unless he was buying a nice bottle from a fine establishment. Some things were worth buying at a high price.

Wendell looked both ways before jaywalking across the street. There wasn't a car in sight. The only company he had was a lost plastic bag, carelessly traveling the currents of wind, just as they did in every stereotypical situation such as this. Wendell decided he would have a drink from the plastic bag before continuing. The expensive soles of his shoes 'clacked' on the pavement as he hurried across the four empty lanes. It made him feel *bad.* There was something special about breaking a pointless law, especially when there was no traffic and there was no reason for him to obey something that literally made no difference.

He had a funny thought that maybe by jaywalking, you were disrupting the flow of reality or something equally dramatic, much like when that one guy stepped on a butterfly in "The Sound of Thunder", and he had altered time and space. As interesting as the concept was, the only backlash he had to worry about was getting a ticket from a police officer who had nothing better to do. But when he arrived on the adjacent sidewalk, he realized that was hogwash and there was no possible way that could logically happen.

Ahead was a dark, shady alley. The passage was well hidden from the city street lights, making it look more like the entrance to a cave. Wendell hadn't taken a back way like this before, but he only lived three parallel streets away. All he had to do was cut through two alleys, and he would be right at his apartment. He looked around the streets behind him; not even the plastic bag was keeping him company now. The night grew eerier the further he got from Leroy's, but it was a nice night indeed.

He looked up and down the two buildings he was about to intersect. They were old structures of weathered brick, just two old buildings struggling to stand the test of time in the city. Compared to the skyscrapers, they seemed old and decrepit. They stood about four or five stories tall; Wendell was feeling a little fuzzy, and the top of the buildings had started to succumb to the darkness of the night. At the very top of the building, Wendell could make out the faint outline of something looking down on him, two massive hands gripping the ledge with stone claws.

Gargoyles, he thought they were called. He wasn't exactly sure how to pronounce the word; he always questioned the vowel sound. Gar-goile? Maybe it was Gargle? Garg-wail? Who knew. Wendell gave a mock salute to the stone statue in the distance and uncapped the bottle to drink to it.

"At ease, soldier!" He laughed to himself and took a swig, feeling the burn once again. It was getting easier now. By the end of the night, it would be like drinking water. Wendell continued to giggle to himself as he entered the alley, leaving the visible safety of the street behind him. It was time to go home.

Wendell made haste into the concrete labyrinth. The darkness didn't bug him, but the filth did. Something about how he knew it hadn't been at least swept in years was all but comforting, and he had just gotten this suit yesterday. Not to mention the thought of getting an old cheeseburger stuck in the tread of his shiny shoes displeased him. He would just have to be in and out and watch where he stepped.

After moments of dark strolling, Wendell could see some lighting ahead. Some of the congested apartments had windows in the alley walls, where a kitchen light or the glow of a television set had let a little glow pool into the blackness ahead. It allowed him to see a dirty heap of newspapers blocking his way, possibly the remnants of a homeless individual's sleeping quarters.

Wendell breathed a sigh of sympathy for his shoes. He could already imagine the roach carcasses and the damp cigarette butts he would track into the lobby. He would be trying to scuff the stale chewing gum off his shoes on the floor mats. It wouldn't look very classy. Maybe he could drop a tip to the clerk, and he wouldn't spread word amongst the other residents.

Wendell tiptoed through the trash in his way, sincerely hoping it wasn't caked with grime. He strolled nice and slow, like navigating through a big bag of soiled leaves. He kept his bottle close, listening to the comforting slosh of booze to ease his tension. The wealthy man was almost through the mess when a tiny shadow burst out from under a stained sale ad, the tarnished images of diamonds and cars fluttering away.

"SQUEEEEEE——" a grungy rat shrieked at him, almost making him soil himself—just as filthy as the trash beneath his feet.

"Ah fuckin—*get!* GET OUT OF HERE!" Wendell shouted at the scuzzy beast, swatting at it pathetically with his bag of liquor. It scurried out of sight, presumably into another home of garbage.

"Oh Jesus, you disgusting, fucking rat!" Wendell shuddered as he caught his breath.

His heart was now running a mile a minute, aggressively thumping against the inside of his chest. Wendell shivered and briefly swatted at himself as he was covered in a whole mob of them, the way you do when you see something you extremely dislike. After that, he tried to laugh it off, but the damage had already been done. He was disgusted and out of his comfort zone. He wasn't far now, though, only a little further to go. He straightened his suit in an effort to reclaim his pride, but was interrupted when somebody called to him from a second-story window.

"Get back to your castle, princess! HA!"

It was some grizzled man in a wife-beater, a beer in one hand and the other pointing while he laughed. This made Wendell angry, and he couldn't help but shout back.

"I'll have you know, sir, that—"

The man slammed the window shut and closed the blinds. Through the diminishing slits of light, Wendell could still see him slapping his leg in humor. Then he was left in the dark once again, alone and embarrassed, ready to be home. Many thoughts raced through his head, mostly angry and degrading thoughts, all aimed towards the laughing man from the window.

Wendell continued to press on, still cursing under his breath. What an asshole. But he knew he had the last laugh, because in the end, Wendell didn't live in a slum, and he had more money. Therefore, he was better. This thought made him feel superior, and he walked on with his chin up a little higher now.

Wendell reached the next street. This one was busier than the previous, but there were still only a few cars passing through in the night. The low and high beams were blinding, and Wendell decided he would behave and walk to the corner and wait for the proper time to cross. This took a few minutes, but he was buzzing nicely and feeling snug. Wendell was still a little shaken by the rat and the rude man, but he tried to pay it no mind. He just stood there waiting for his signal, only stopping briefly to check his watch. It was 9:22 p.m.

When he looked up from his watch, he was rewarded with the glowing mid-stride stick figure. Wendell crossed the street correctly this time, wading through the bright headlights of the waiting vehicles. His buzz was settling in nicely, and the vodka was doing a good job of loosening him up. It required effort to keep good posture without sloppy steps. Wendell kept his back straight and strolled down the sidewalk, doing everything in his power to keep his cool. The last thing he needed was an officer stopping him and cuffing him for public intoxication. He was sure he would blow over the legal limit.

There was only one more alleyway to get through before he would reach his building. He looked into the darkness of what seemed like a tunnel. The way the buildings cut off all light from the streets was intimidating. He could just barely see the glow on the other side, the welcoming lights of the fancy apartments he stayed at. It was a beacon of the upper crust, just outside the run-down murk of poverty. *This alley had to be at least a little cleaner*, he thought. It was so close to the nicer side of the city.

Feeling fearless from his booze, he descended into the darkness, focusing on the building on the other side. Wendell looked up to see the same kind of statue from before, looming over him with eyes and wings of stone. It was identical to the one before. He wondered how he had never noticed such things before. He thought statues like this were only posted on the courthouse buildings or something of the sort. It almost seemed like a warning. Wendell laughed and took a final drink, thinking of it as a boost to make the home stretch.

After a few strides, it was like the alley had swallowed him. All the bustling noise from the streets was dampened to a near silence, with only the faint *beep* of the occasional honking horn. It was all replaced by the *hum* of more air conditioners and the unmistakable smell of trash. Dumpsters lined the wall on his left, nasty, sweating metal heaps that he could only imagine what rodents hid inside. He didn't understand how people could live with those things being right next to their windows. One thing he knew now, of course, was that his shoes would have to be thrown away. He decided he would get replacements first thing in the morning.

Wendell's foot struck a can, and he jumped at the unexpectedly loud noise. The dented can skittered across the pavement, echoing as it tumbled away. Wendell was too busy watching the can that he almost bumped into one of the dumpsters, and he awkwardly stumbled to avoid the jutting mass. As he avoided the bin, his shoulder bumped something else, something that pushed him *back.* He looked to see another man, his face masked by a hooded sweatshirt. A lit cigarette hung from his lips, the burning cherry glowing. It was the only thing he could make out in the light.

"Shit—sorry. Didn't see you there. Almost tripped," Wendell chuckled awkwardly, brushing off his suit.

The hooded man just stood there, looking at him. Wendell looked around, hoping he was staring at someone else, but there wasn't anyone else around. Just as he was about to mind his own business and make a quick exit, the hooded man spoke, a deep voice calling him out in the creeping dark.

"Whatcha' drinkin' there, friend?" The voice was rough, *mean.* The hooded man took a step forward, and Wendell took it as a sign he should take his leave.

"Well, I best be going. Got a big day tomorrow," he excused himself, turning on his heel to make a quick getaway. He scurried away from the hooded man, wanting to put as much distance as he could before getting home. He looked again for the apartment building's glow, only thirty feet away now. He felt hope that he would make it home safe and focus on the important things, like getting new shoes that would match his suit. But now two more figures were stepping out of the shadows, obscuring his view of the glow that meant safety.

Fuck.

One of the men ahead was chuckling, looking just as dangerous as the one he bumped into. With a spreading panic, Wendell looked behind him to see that the hooded man was following as well. He was dragging a pipe at his side, letting it bounce along the dumpsters as he came closer. A coarse laugh was escaping his lips, and one of the guys behind him was howling weirdly, almost like a cat-call. The hooded man spoke again, this time banging the pipe loudly on the broad side of the dumpster.

"I *said,* whatcha' drinkin', friend? Whatcha' got in that bag there?" He was close now, giving off a heavy scent of beer and cigarette smoke. The burning cherry glowed, showing the mixture of piercings and tattoos that made up the man's face. Wendell thought of the bottle in his hand, and he held it close. It was the only thing he had to defend himself. Surely it would work as a weapon.

"I don't want any trouble. Just trying to get home." Wendell said. He could feel himself shaking as the three of them drew closer.

"Is it tequila? I love me some tequila," The hooded man inquired, taking a big drag from his smoke. He exhaled in Wendell's face and flicked the cigarette at him. With a burst of sparks, he frantically swatted it off his suit. Wendell cursed and looked around for someone to help him, but no one was there.

"What—what the hell's wrong with you?!" Wendell yelled, angry that some of the ash had burned his hand. Why couldn't these assholes just leave him alone?

"Plenty of things..," said the hooded man and gave him a hard shove in the chest. Wendell stumbled back weakly from the force that seemed to take his breath away.

"Whoa there, stranger! You'll lose your footing!" yelled one of them behind him, shoving him harder. Wendell tripped and fell forward, face-first into the alley's filth. The men laughed, whooping loudly like a bunch of teenage boys. Some of the grime from the floor got into Wendell's mouth, and he coughed and spit to get it out. The nasty shit was in his teeth. God knew what kind of muck was matted into the concrete.

"Please, I have money. Just leave me alone!" pleaded Wendell. He felt like an ant amongst giants with microscopes. The hooded one kept banging on the dumpsters while the others hooted and hollered.

"*Oh yeah*, that's a good start. Let's see it," said the hooded man, who gave him a swift kick in the ribs. Wendell writhed on the floor like a beaten dog, covering his face as they all started to kick him. Their boots and shoes pelted his legs and shoulders, raining down like concrete hail.

"H-HELP! *I'M BEING MUGGED!*" shouted Wendell, and all of them laughed. There were apartment windows open in the alley. Wendell hoped that in one of them, someone was listening, maybe someone would call the police. He saw someone approach one of the windows, and for a second, he felt a flicker of hope.

"Please, help!" he cried, but to his surprise, the only person who looked out the window slammed theirs shut. As he reached for them, they closed the curtains and shut off the lights. There was nobody to help him as the boots started raining down.

There were so many feet assaulting him that he couldn't keep track; every time he went to shield himself, a steel toe would catch his forehead or stomach, and one even hit him square between the legs. Wendell gasped and coughed and cried out in pain, the pain in his testicles and stomach making him want to puke. But still he held onto the bottle, cradling it like a glass baby.

"Alright, alright. Let the man get his money," said the hooded man. Suddenly, the kicking stopped, and he could finally breathe. As Wendell squirmed to climb to his feet, one of the men behind him stomped on the back of his thigh, giving him a horrible charley horse. They all laughed together as he cried out in pain.

With shaking limbs, Wendell worked his way to his hands and knees. His body hurt all over. He could feel where every kick had landed, where the nasty bruises would form. There was a disgusting grit in his teeth that only got worse with the taste of blood. Wendell hacked and spit, but he couldn't get it out of his mouth. There was a hot trickle from his nose, and he realized he was now in tears.

"Come on now, baby. Don't keep us waiting. Let's see that money," demanded the leader, pulling off his hood. His hair was shaved in decorated strips with immaculate, alternating braids. It was odd-looking hair, but it seemed to match his intimidating face.

"A-alright, just don't kick me anymore!" Wendell begged, trying to get back on his feet. The men took a step back to give him some room, but through the haze of his vision, he could still feel them lingering like a pack of dogs. His joints shook as he pushed himself up, his entire body singing with pain. The men behind him did some kind of fist-bump handshake, while the leader lit another cigarette.

Wendell looked up at his cocky, stupidly tattooed face. The cigarette hanging in his lips with his distasteful piercings. The way they mercilessly beat him and bullied him angered him so much that he clenched his teeth. The filth shaved against the enamel, the horrid taste that was there because of them. He was covered in his own blood and possibly feces for all he knew, and now he was crying like a child. All of this abuse—and now he was going to give them *money.* Wendell gripped the neck of the bottle in his hand, the other wiping his nose with a dirty sleeve.

"Let's go, princess. I don't have all night," said Tattoo-face, sucking on his cigarette. Once again, he exhaled the smoke on Wendell.

"I don't know how much I have on me, but—"

"Give me the *fucking* wallet, now!" he barked, banging the pipe on the dumpster. Wendell flinched, cowering in fear.

"Okay, *okay.* I'm getting it, alright? Fuck!" shouted Wendell, shaking in his ruined shoes. His seven-hundred-dollar suit was trashed, stained and ripped beyond repair. His hair was a disheveled mess, and there was rat shit in his mouth. He was humiliated.

Slowly, Wendell reached his free hand to his back pocket, his dirty fingers gripping his wallet. He felt defeated as he pulled it free, knowing the dozens of hundred-dollar bills were about to be pissed away, and all these men had to do was beat him for it. It didn't matter that the money was just change to him; it was the *principle* of it, and Wendell found that more infuriating than the fact that they had beaten him and ruined his suit. Wendell looked at the tattoo man and wondered if they were going to kill him. Wendell held the wallet out weakly, keeping the bottle at his side.

"There we go. See? That wasn't so bad now, was it?" askeds Tattoo-face, grabbing the wallet.

With all the strength Wendell could muster, he swung the bottle of vodka like a billy club, aiming for the man's face. He felt an exhilaration in standing up for himself, in handing out some personal justice to the man who was trying to take his money. To let them know that even if they could beat him up, they fucked with the wrong guy. This all went down the drain, however, when he realized Tattoo-face had caught the bottle in a giant hand with no visible effort.

"Oh, you fucked up. You fucked up *bad," he said*, right before driving his knee into Wendell's gut.

The force lifted Wendell off the ground, and as all his air left him, so did the contents of his stomach. Vomit splashed on the ground below him, violently ejected from his burning throat against his will. Even though he was under the influence, it didn't keep him from feeling like complete shit. The men laughed at his retching, even as their leader held him up by his collar. He was strong as hell, holding him in place with just one hand as he weakly bobbed from side to side.

"You got some balls, pretty boy!" he yelled, shaking him hard. Bile still bubbled on Wendell's lips, and he muttered something inaudible.

"What's that? I can't hear you!" Tattoo-face taunted and savagely head-butted him, slamming his inked forehead between Wendell's eyes.

Wendell had never broken his nose before, but he was sure now that it was. His world went black momentarily, only to see his vision angle towards the sky. Wendell fell backwards, blood running down his face and onto his soiled suit. He waited for the impact of the cement, but it never came. Both men behind him snatched him up, each holding an arm to keep him upright. Wendell's legs buckled, and he threw up again, another burning mass of alcohol scorching the back of his throat. The broken pressure in his face only made it worse.

The leader was going through his wallet now, searching through every fold for any form of currency. The vodka bottle and pipe were held in the crook of his arm lazily. He found the bills and tossed the wallet at Wendell, which bounced off his chin and fell to the ground. He counted the money, shuffling the bills one at a time while puffing on his cigarette.

"I gotta say, champ, this is a lot of money. You must be a pretty important guy," said Tattoo-face, wadding up the cash and shoving it in the pocket of his jeans. Wendell mumbled again, bubbling more broken words in a mess of spit.

"What's that, pretty boy? Can't quite hear you, your face is a little fucked up," he teased, uncapping the bottle and taking a long swig.

"Go fuck yourself," Wendell spat, squirming in the robber's grasp, "You're shit, you know that? You're *nothing*. I step on pieces of shit like you every day. I could *buy* you," he continued, his own drunken rage making him laugh.

"Don't worry, punk, tonight's on you. You're gonna buy all my drinks tonight, probably even the bitch I take home after-wards."

Wendell blinked at him, squinting through the blood and sweat that nearly blinded him. He cleared his throat with a disgust-ing rattle of phlegm and spat in his face. The nasty glob stuck to the man's tattooed cheek, and Wendell felt the immediate reward of the pipe. The elbow-piece at the end dug so far into his stomach he wondered if he would throw up a third time. With a groan, Wendell hunched over, but one of his captors grabbed a fistful of his hair to make him look at the leader.

"Watch this one, boys, it's gonna be good. One for the books," the leader said, wiping the spit from his cheek. He took a final swig of the vodka and tossed the bottle into the air, readying the pipe like a bat. Wendell watched the open bottle tumble skyward, the crystalline liquid sloshing like a fountain. With a solid homerun swing, the bottle exploded into a wild spray of glass and booze that hit Wendell like a shotgun blast. The liquor got in his eyes, and the glass stung his face; some of the shrapnel even went into his mouth. It was amazing how something so clear and beautiful could burn so badly.

Wendell screamed and thrashed to cover his eyes. One of the men howled and gave him an elbow in the back, sending him blindly sprawling once again. On the ground, Wendell wiped at his face, but his hands were filthy and covered in booze as well. There was no way to effectively get it out of his eyes. All he could do was suffer through the sting. He felt a kick in his ribs, and it tossed him into the front of the nearest dumpster, which he found himself cowering against. He huddled against the metal wall, covering his face as he waited for the next blow.

"Well, this was fun. But I've about had enough. Let's finish this bitch," said Tattoo-face, propping Wendell up against the dumpster. He tossed the pipe and reached behind his back, pulling out a chrome pistol that seemed to shine even in the dark. He shoved the barrel in Wendell's mouth, looking him in the eyes as he choked on the gun. The steel was cold in his mouth, and he could taste the oil on his tongue.

"W-wait, you're gonna kill him?" piped up one of the other thugs, suddenly uncertain of the turn of events.

"Yeah, what the hell, man? He's had enough! We got the money. Let's split!" the other pleaded, but their leader just looked at them angrily.

"Nah, I don't think so. You heard the man! He steps on shit like me *every day,*" he seethed. He had an angry grin of piercings like some sort of metal monster.

"Yeah, but come on, man. Look at him, he's done. Let's go," they pleaded, looking around now to see if anyone was watching t hem.

Wendell just closed his eyes and let them argue, all the pain in his body singing from the abuse. He just tried to tone them out, listening to the noises of the city, just in case it would be his last time. In the distance, he heard screeching tires and honking horns, the bustling of traffic that could be heard anywhere you go. The stinging in his eyes burrowed deeply, but he ignored it. He just focused on the breeze hitting his face and the sounds of the wind, things that would carry him into the afterlife once the tattooed pig put a bullet in his head. In his temporary bliss, he heard something strange, like an irregular gust in the air. He tried to focus on it, but the men in front of him were getting louder.

"Shut the fuck up!" yelled the Tattooed man, the gun still stuffed in Wendell's mouth, "I'm the one who calls the shots here, you got that? You don't like it, then fuckin' go. I'll keep your share if you don't got the balls," he said, and the other two thugs quieted down. One scratched his head before speaking again.

"Alright, alright. Just make this quick so we can get out of here," he conceded, obediently, before bowing his head in shame.

"That's what I thought. Sweet dreams, cock-sucker," said Tattoo face, pulling the hammer back. Wendell imagined the bullet, primed and ready to go, and wondered if it was going to hurt at all. Would he feel anything from it? How long would he be conscious with a hole in his forehead? He swallowed hard, his main regret being that he was going to die in such a filthy place. Why couldn't it be a little cleaner?

WHOOSH. WHOOSH. WHOOSH.

"What the hell is that noise?" one of the thugs whispered, squinting to make out whatever it was. Tattoo man looked over his shoulder, and a second later, he was violently lifted off the ground. Wendell felt the gun leave his mouth, and he opened his eyes in time to see his abuser writhing in midair.

WHOOSH. WHOOSH.

A very large, dark figure was holding Tattoo-face with massive arms, dangling him in the air like a child. Together they bounced with every beat of giant wings, so big they sent a gust of air at the ground with every flap. Tattoo-face was trying to point his gun at it, but it seemed to overpower him effortlessly with arms full of bulging muscle. The monster's hands were three times the size of a human's hands, and they squeezed so hard you could hear the crunching of bone. The man screamed in pain, and the other thugs gasped, cowering in fright under the airborne beast. Wendell just watched dumbfounded, transfixed on the thing that seemed impossible to exist.

The hulking monster stared at them from above with glowing red eyes. Wicked horns protruded through the sides of its head, next to long, pointed ears. Its face was emotionless, bearing large, dagger-like teeth that protruded from its underbite. Wendell felt an emptying pit in his stomach as he recognized the monster.

It was the gargoyle from the first alleyway he went through. He didn't know if he had provoked it by saluting it, but for whatever reason, it was staring not at the other thugs, but at *him.*

Dear God.

A menacing shriek erupted from the winged beast's lips, so loud the windows around them began to crack. Tattoo-face shot wildly, sending bullets in all directions while he was stuck in the torturous cradle. He screamed at the monster, mostly just a scramble of curse words, but suddenly his words were turned into an agonized wail. With flexing gray muscles, the monster tore him in half diagonally. A red burst erupted from the torn torso, showering everyone with a splash of hot blood. Wendell watched in pure terror as it hefted both pieces above its horned head like trophies. In one fist, it held one shoulder, the left arm, half a torso, and both kicking legs. The other held the remaining shoulder, head, and the right arm with the smoking gun. The tattoo-man's face was petrified with an expression of eternal anguish. The gargoyle tossed the pieces away, painting the bricks with gushing arterial spray. Beating its massive wings, it reared back, as if it was going to dive in Wendell's direction.

"Holy shit, oh-my-god, run!" shouted one of the thugs, who stopped to pick up the pipe from the ground, before making a run for it. With his second step, he slipped on the broken glass, eating shit on the concrete in an awkward mess.

"Shit-shit-shit—" swore the other, pulling a bulky firearm from underneath his windbreaker. Wendell had seen one before in a pawn shop. It was smaller than a rifle but had a large, skinny magazine. It was a nasty-looking piece.

Wendell shielded his eyes as the thug lit up the alley with his MAC-10, spraying a flurry of bullets and muzzle-flashes in the monster's direction. The gargoyle covered itself with a single giant wing, acting as a veiny cloak. The rounds deflected off the bullet-proof shield, ricocheted off the surrounding bricks and *pinged* off the dumpsters. Wendell watched the unstoppable fiend shrug off the bullets until the thug's firearm 'clicked' empty. The panicking thug looked at the gun as if it betrayed him, and the gargoyle peeked over its wing, casting a glow with its red eyes. The thug tossed the gun, and it clattered away into the darkness.

"Ah—FUCK YOU! I'm not scared of you!" shouted the mugger, giving it the finger before turning to run away. The gargoyle shrieked and bolted for him, gliding fast on his heels. The dark mass flew over Wendell's head, and he felt the gentle wisp of what he thought was a tail graze his hair. In the confusion, he climbed to his feet, just in time to see the monster descend on his prey.

The winged beast swooped down to the thug and snatched him up, grabbing the entirety of the man's head in one massive hand. The man screamed through the slits of the monster's giant fingers, and he was helplessly pulled upward. With heavy gusts, the wings flapped again to gain altitude.

A little voice in Wendell's head told him to run. It took a few seconds for his legs to obey, but he started moving, slowly and stupidly at first, but moving nonetheless. With the beast being temporarily distracted, he knew it was his only opportunity to escape. There was an electricity surging within him, so sudden and intoxicating that his legs seemed to move on their own. Even after accepting defeat from the muggers earlier, the sudden turn of events had changed his mind. He wanted to *live.*

The other thug was still trying to get on his feet, slipping repeatedly on the shards of broken glass from the destroyed vodka bottle. The gargoyle was rising now, carrying the screaming man higher and higher until they were parallel with the second-story windows. Wendell darted underneath them, hoping to God the tail wouldn't swipe at him. He was sprinting now, right passed the other thug struggling to get up. He focused on the doors of his apartment building, gunning for the guiding light. It seemed so far away, like the alley would never end.

"HEY! Don't leave me here!" shouted the thug, but Wendell didn't even bother to look.

Above, the gargoyle smashed the squirming thug's head into the wall, *grinding* the bone into the masonry. It was a horrible, sickening sound, like someone dragging a broken watermelon across gravel. The thug fell silent, but the monster wasn't pleased until after it hefted the body above its head and thrust its hand through the man's chest. The monster's claws were angled inward like a spear tearing through paper, not stopping until they protruded from his back. The beast heaved the limp body into the dumpster with a loud crash.

The vast wings went slack, and the monster started to glide again, like an arrow shooting straight for Wendell and the other mugger. The two of them glanced back in unison, just as it smoothly transitioned from the air to the ground. It hit the concrete running, breaking into a sprint on all fours, its tail whipping behind it. Wendell's vision was blurred, but he shoved on as hard as he could, pushing his bruised legs as for all they were worth. The mugger was a few paces behind, and the monstrosity was gaining fast.

The beast's claws scraped the asphalt, a terrifying rhythm that seemed to inch closer and closer on their tail. The monster grunted with every stride, a strange metallic hiss that almost sounded robotic. Wendell was closing his eyes now, the streetlights so close he could touch them. He felt that if he could just get out of the darkness of the alley, he would be safe. He kept pushing, his lungs empty and his body pleading for it to end. *Just a little further*, he told himself. *Just a little further.*

Only a few feet from the sidewalk, the monstrosity let out a final piercing metallic howl, breaking into a dive with its enlarged hands stretched out. Wendell looked over his shoulder to see it tackle the remaining mugger to the ground. He was so transfixed on the beast that he didn't even realize he had made it onto the street. Behind him, they tumbled to a halt in a mess of swiping claws and blurred red eyes. The thug swung the pipe in a desperate attempt to defend himself, but the beast caught the weapon in its mouth, smashing through the steel with its stone teeth. Its grand wings fanned out like a falling curtain descended over its prey, shielding it from everything except the deadly mauling.

Wendell watched from the street as darkness enveloped them until he could see nothing except the glowing red eyes. The safety of the streetlights shone on him as he stood there catching his breath. He was gasping and barely standing, but he had made it. Next to him, there was a screaming of tires and a blaring horn, and a new light that nearly blinded him.

Wendell flinched as the car hit him, not lethally, but enough to make him stumble onto the hood. The bumper hit his hip, and his body fell forward, and he raised his arms in time to cushion the impact from the hood. Dizzily, he picked himself up, but his attention wasn't on the car. He looked to the alley.

The glowing red eyes were gone, the alleyway empty. He had made it.

"Hey! What the fuck's your problem, man?! I coulda' killed you!" shouted the driver of the yellow cab, angrily inching himself out of the window.

Wendell was dumbfounded, and he looked back and forth between the driver and the alley, saying the only thing he could muster:

"Uh... what?"

The driver looked insulted. With a scowl, he unbuckled his seatbelt and opened the door.

"Hey, asshole! What's your problem? Get out of the road!" said the driver, holding up traffic behind him. Other horns started sounding from the line that was immediately backed up behind them.

Wendell was silent for a moment, then started laughing hysterically with his hands in the air.

"I'm alive," he said, almost dumbfounded.

"What the hell is wrong with you? You bleedin'?" The driver's anger was starting to evolve into concern, but he was still very obviously inconvenienced.

"I'M ALIVE! YES!" shouted Wendell, grabbing the driver's coat and shaking him excitedly. The driver raised his eyebrows and awkwardly pulled away. Wendell let go and continued to cross the street, laughing through the tears that burned in his eyes. The creeping fear of the alleyway monster started to fade, replaced by pure astounded surprise.

It didn't matter now. He was home.

"Uh, man, gross!" the driver wiped at his coat, at the scuffs left behind from Wendell's dirty hands. He stood there for a moment, confused, before cursing and getting back into his car. The cab driver pulled away, and traffic resumed, the busy street picking up as if nothing had happened. Under the blanket of city noises, a chewed piece of bloody pipe rolled out of the darkness of the alley.

Wendell pushed his way through the entrance of the expensive apartment building and was greeted by the man behind the desk. A man he knew as Joel, if his memory was still intact. The clerk was obviously repulsed by Wendell's condition, backing away from the counter like he was made out of bees or something.

Wendell tried to play it smooth, but he was a wreck. The shell shock was starting to settle in, and Wendell felt the adrenaline waning as the minutes dragged on. He spoke in broken sentences and made wild hand gestures. He explained that he didn't have his keys or any form of identification—due to his lost wallet. He started explaining what happened to him, but he was stuttering, and the words wouldn't come together.

It was hard to swing a believable story when you were covered in blood and broken glass and smelled like a knocked-over mini bar. Each attempt to convince Joel only yielded the same response—a soundless, quick nod with a blank, open mouth. When all else failed, Wendell promised a generous tip in exchange for his cooperation. Eventually, the clerk gave in and provided him with a replacement room key, charging the credit card on file. Whether it was because of the tip he mentioned or just the fact that he wanted him to go away before the scene got any worse, he didn't know.

Wendell gave his thanks and departed quickly, desperately wanting to get to the safety of the hotel room. He hastily entered the elevator, ready to get cleaned up and leave this night behind him.

As the cabin rode up, Wendell couldn't help but think of the monster. He couldn't help but feel the creature's stare. Hear the metallic scream. It echoed over and over in his head, and even with the doors pressed shut, he felt like he would see them puncture the steel at any moment and pry the doors apart. Glowing eyes, curved horns, and bulletproof wings. It had torn the men apart like *toys,* tearing through them like they were nothing but an inconvenience. As the floors climbed through the tens and twenties, he wondered how he was fortunate enough to get away. If the encounter had been real at all. The burning in his eyes and the aches in his body told him otherwise, but he couldn't help but have his doubts. The encounter was not of this world, end of story.

Wendell was so overcome with thought and exhaustion that he was startled by the opening of the elevator doors. He flinched and threw his hands up in defense against the claws and the deafening scream. With his eyes squeezed shut and clenched teeth, he waited for the stone daggers to tear at his throat, but it never came. Hesitantly, he opened his eyes to see there was no monster, only a confused gentleman and a giggling mistress. Wendell lowered his guard in embarrassment once again. He was growing quite tired of his own mental shenanigans.

"Sorry. Been a long night, I'm afraid," apologized Wendell, scratching at his matted scalp.

The man was in a three-piece suit, complete with a shining pocket watch. The bleach-blonde mistress was wearing an expensive, glittering cocktail dress that overly exposed the sides of her breasts. It was exactly what one would expect to find at the very top of the building—the penthouse suites on the forty-first floor.

"It certainly appears that way. Doesn't it, honey?" said the gentleman.

Wendell got out, and together the couple walked around him with condescending looks. The blonde woman giggled while toying with her necklace of pearls, and the gentleman checked his pocket watch, avoiding his gaze until the elevator doors shielded him from their view.

Sometimes, even Wendell couldn't stand the rich.

There were only three suites on this floor; Wendell's was the first door on his right. He fumbled with his key card, trying to keep his filthy hands from contaminating it. It took a few times to get the green light, but once he did, he shoved his way in quickly and closed the door behind him for good. He engaged every lock on the door, even going to the extent of wedging a chair under the knob to ensure nobody could get in.

The luxurious penthouse suite was a hidden gem placed high above the poverty and ruggedness of the city streets. It was furnished with very impressive, handcrafted furniture and comfortable lighting that always allowed Wendell to settle in right. Genuine sculptures and paintings lined every wall, and the whole retreat was complete with a balcony that overlooked the whole city. Wendell never thought a night like this would come, where he would use it to hide from the world. For once, he didn't want anyone to know where he was.

Wendell was already shrugging out of his ruined jacket and kicking off his shoes. He wanted the clothes out of his sight and removed from existence as soon as humanly possible. The suit and shoes were tattered and would only serve as a reminder of what had transpired. He thought if he could just clean himself up and remove the evidence, it would go away. After all, he was the only one who survived the encounter, and he thought that if he forgot it ever happened, maybe it would get chalked up to everyday gang violence. He imagined the monster wouldn't be paying a visit to the police station any time soon; maybe the whole thing would just disappear.

The clothes were soon stuffed in the bag and thrown in the trash. Even though he was starting to get used to the stinging in the cuts on his face and his eyes, he was still longing to be cleansed of the madness. He ran a hot shower in the immaculate bathroom and looked at himself in the mirror as the water warmed up. He looked like hell. Bruises from head to toe, at least a dozen cuts, including a split lip and eyebrow. There was still a piece of glass stuck in his cheek, and when he removed the shard, it only added to the blood that had painted him. He opened the medicine cabinet and observed the rainy-day stash of not-so-legal pharmaceuticals. He grabbed a few painkillers and muscle relaxers, then walked to the kitchen to find something to wash them down. He decided one of his many two-hundred-dollar vodkas would have to be opened for the first time. After the pills were swallowed, he took a couple of extra pulls in celebration of still being alive.

The shower was too hot, but he didn't care. He stood in the cascade and let the scalding spray burn away all that had clung to him. His cuts burned from the liquid fire, but it soothed his muscles, and in time, he was actually starting to feel better. He decided that first thing tomorrow morning, he would cancel all appointments and devote the day to replacing the lost suit. It would give him some time to look more approachable and get his shit together. He was thinking pinstripe, maybe a new pair of wing tips, but he wasn't sure just yet.

Wendell killed the water and toweled off, already feeling the high from his drugs. It would be a nice send-off for the night. He made his way to the bedroom, drying off and sipping from the new bottle of vodka as he went. In the back of his mind, he was disappointed that he had paid top dollar for a nice bottle that was only to be shattered, but in time, he hoped he would forget about that as well. He dressed slowly, going with silk pajamas so they would be less abrasive on his damaged skin. He was feeling better now that he was clean.

Thoughts of the dark alley continued to brew in his mind, but he just kept pushing them away, drinking from the bottle every time he saw those red eyes or heard those beating wings. After going through almost half of the new bottle, he started telling himself that he *was* robbed, but they took his money, and out of the decency of their hearts, they let him go, and everyone went on their merry way. He started to believe it too, and as he crawled into bed and sloppily pulled the covers over himself, he decided the suit would be dark gray, and maybe he would go the extra mile for shark-skin loafers. He drifted off to sleep, thinking of the fresh dress socks he would be pulling onto his feet.

Wendell awoke to a loud *thud*. He jolted up quickly, immediately regretting the swift movement. A groan immediately followed, as the pain poked through his sedation. He was groggy but completely alert, looking around for the source of the disturbance, unknowingly gripping the vodka bottle by the neck for the second time in the same night. It was dark, silent. He looked at his watch; he had only slept for twenty minutes. A cold sweat had collected on his brow, and he wiped at it, swallowing back a nervous churn that was twisting in the pit of his stomach. He tried to think of where the noise came from. It sounded more like it came from outside rather than something out in the hall. He sat there for what felt like a frozen eternity, not sure whether to get up or hide under the covers and pretend it was just his imagination. He was craning his head, listening to the wind outside. Surely he had just imagined it. Just as he sighed and started to lean back into the comfort of his king-size bed, there was another noise, so clear in the night he knew it hadn't been a dream. It was a creaking whine, like bending steel or someone opening a rusted car door. And it was coming from o utside.

The balcony.

With his vision distorted from sleep, Wendell looked outside the bedroom window, seeing nothing but the extending city landscape. Nothing out of the ordinary, at least nothing he could see. Wendell tossed the covers and swung out of bed, almost falling as he tried to stand. His legs shook, and his feet struggled to find his slippers in the dark. Bottle in hand, he left the bedroom and began his brave walk down the hall.

He was tired of running for the night. As much as he wanted to believe it was just a bird hitting the slider, he knew it was something more sinister. He had his chance to get away and clean up, and this was as far as the road would take him. He guessed sometimes a man can't run from his destiny; it finds *them.*

Wendell stood at the end of the hallway, taking a deep breath before rounding the corner into full view of the balcony. He heard the winding groan again, but it was louder now that he was closer and wide awake. He adjusted his grip on the bottleneck and walked into the living room, slowly so he wouldn't bump into the furniture. When he looked through the glass sliding door, he could see it clear as day, looming like a shadow, completely still in the night. The metal balcony railing was bent downward as it supported the weight of the dead load. Quietly perched on top was the Gargoyle, patiently waiting.

For a time, Wendell just stood there, unable to look away from the intimidating beast. It was moving ever so slightly, its massive shoulders rising and falling as it breathed. It was looking right at him, its glowing eyes now a light shade of blue that lit up the entire living room. The monster's massive wings were slack, resting over its body like a large cloak, with two miniature claws interlocked to keep it in place. Underneath its wings, he could see its pointy elbows, propped elegantly on its knees in its perpetual perch. It looked just like the statue he saw earlier that night, so still and peaceful, he could swear it was solid stone. Compared to ferocity in the alleyway, at least this time it had the decency to wait and let Wendell accept his fate on his own terms.

Wendell approached the slider, feeling as if every step was bringing him closer to his death. The monster waited, watching as he crossed the living room, the bright blue eyes piercing his soul. When he came to the slider, he unlocked it and, after swallowing hard, he pulled it open. Cool wind whistled past him and flooded the apartment, along with the sound of the beast's breathing. It was like a low growl, like little gears powering a machine with every breath. Wendell looked into the glowing eyes as he stepped out onto the balcony, face to face with the demon he had previously watched rip several men to pieces. For what seemed like forever, they just stood there, looking at each other, the sounds of the city life echoing a thousand feet below. Despite his overwhelming fear, it was Wendell who broke the silence.

"Why?" he said, the sound of his own voice chilling him.

The Gargoyle just inclined its head, its long-wicked ears twitching as it pondered. Wendell waited as it said nothing, wondering how soon it was going to snatch him up and tear him apart, tossing his limbs to the streets below. He would stand no chance, he knew that. He just hoped it wouldn't be as bad as he thought it was going to be.

Alas, the monster moved, so dreadfully slow all Wendell could to was hold his breath as its huge wings shifted, flowing like tarps in the wind. However, it didn't attack him; it just reached out one of its enlarged hands, a clenched fist that stopped just inches from Wendell's chest. Wendell gasped, his whole body shaking as it froze again. He wasn't sure what to do, so he just stood there, not wanting to upset the monster that dwarfed him. He just looked at the giant fist, then back to the glowing eyes, fearing any move would render him into bloody pieces. The Gargoyle's ears twitched again, and the giant fist nudged him. Wendell fought the urge to scream but realized something that didn't quite make sense to him. It was *holding* something. Something it wanted him to take.

Wendell reached a hand up, palm to the sky, as he positioned it under the monster's giant hand. The Gargoyle huffed and uncurled his fingers, and something wet and clammy plopped into his hand. Without as much as a sound, the beast nodded its head and stretched out its wings. With a single flap, it pushed off the balcony with its bent hind legs, taking flight on the whistling wind. Wendell watched it soar over the rooftops of the city, and in mere seconds, it was gone, vanishing into the shadows of the night.

Wendell stood there alone, speechless. For a while, he simply stood there, lingering by the bent rails. Up so high, all he could hear was the wind and the busy city below. A symphony of honking cars and sirens. He wondered if they were heading to the alleyway, if someone had actually called the police.

Wendell took a deep breath and embraced it all. In time, he even found himself smiling a little. The leather bifold was roughed up, stained with blood, and reeked of alcohol. But he could still make out the cursive 'W' stamped into the side.

OLD MAN

Grundale's feet ached. Every time his fur shoes touched the frozen earth, he felt the inescapable creep of the cold work its way into his soles. Fluffy white snow had started to collect around his ankles, crusting over his wool trousers and applying an icy burn to his skin. The only warmth came from the torches behind him, held by the men who urged him forward. He longed for heat. When the Watchmen kicked down the door to his cottage and took him into custody, they only allowed him to garb in his fur coat and shoes, leaving him to shiver in his breeches. It wasn't nearly enough to fight against the chill of winter, and as they pushed him through the night, he swore he could feel frost collecting on his old bones.

Although it mattered not—his life wasn't their concern. A noose waited in town with his name on it.

An elderly man of seventy years, Grundale was no murderer. With Bloodletter as his family name, he was a true warrior in his prime. Many had tussled with him on the battlefield long ago, and those close enough to witness the flash of his steel didn't live to tell the tale. But his tired hands hadn't touched the hilt of a sword in over two decades; the blade remained sheathed so he could live quietly as a hermit. He had spent the remainder of his years whittling and hunting game in the wooded land, leaving a life of rampant bloodshed behind him for good.

The accusations against him had brought nothing but anger and confusion, and when his captors stormed his home, with glazed eyes and breath foul with drink, they ignored his pleas of innocence. When he refused to oblige and confess, the rugged men beat him and spat in his face, dragging him out into the winter cold despite his ravings of innocence.

Sentenced to hang until he took his last breath, Grundale was marching to his end, charged with the abduction and murder of two young children: a boy and his sister. The small town in which they lived had become outraged and sent a party to bring him in, to see him swing at dawn's first light. No amount of reasoning could sway the men. They were determined to see him hang. Some seemed giddy with excitement over it.

But Grundale was an innocent man, or so he swore.

The fierce wind whipped at his unbuttoned coat, stinging his wrinkled skin and freezing the tears that streamed down his cheeks. Fear welled in his gut, and his thin hands shook. The rope binding his wrists chafed the skin raw, and his hands swelled from the lack of circulation. He fought to loosen it, but it only seemed to worsen the bind, making the rope dig deeper and wind tighter. The pain shot up his arms in bursts as every frayed fiber dug into the meat. His bony fingers ached from the constriction, protesting the amber ring he wore on his pinky.

Behind him, the men cursed him and tossed back their bottles, the piercing scent of their booze hot on the wind. Their drink fed their anger like wildfire, and he could feel them boiling more with every swig they took. Grundale swallowed, his throat dry and coarse from the winter air. Every wheezing breath shriveled his throat. The aches and pains in his limbs seemed to throb in the cold, and he fought to keep focus on his feet beneath him. His feet were weak, his steps clumsy.

The old man wondered how far they had walked. He felt like he had been pushing ahead all through the night, but the trees all looked the same in the dark. He had traveled and hunted in these familiar woods for dozens of years, keeping track of every rotting tree and young sapling as his years passed in the wilderness. But the trees looked different now. He felt lost—lost in the fear of what was to come—the fear of death. Every twisted trunk seemed to watch him struggle from the shadows, like they had turned their backs on him after all this time. He thought of escaping, but at his age, he knew he wouldn't stand a chance. The Watchmen were numb and determined in their march. Most of them were young and muscular, garbed in scarves and mittens and thick coats. They were cozy in their many layers, while he could barely keep his clothes from falling off his shivering frame. He wouldn't get as far as two strides before he collapsed from his own fatigue, only for them to beat him more.

One of the men took a long swallow from his bottle and smacked his lips, then cleared his throat to speak.

"There's a special place in hell for you, old man!"

The others chimed in, hurling more insults at him.

"You're a twisted bastard, Bloodletter!"

"Swing in the wind, you will!"

Once a respected member of the community, these insults saddened him. He bowed his head as their insults grew viler, their words stinging just as much as the air that burned his cheeks. People used to look up to him. They used to ask him for advice, have him over for dinner. He had met and helped many families in the past, teaching some to hunt and forage when they were younger. The seasons were harsh here, and being the eldest woodsman, they would often seek his guidance. He tried to focus on the kind words of the past, but he couldn't hear them now. They were drowned out by the hate they spat.

Grundale looked up to see a crow landing on a tree's branch. It ruffled its feathers and cocked its head to the side, staring down at him with its beady black eyes. Its gaze was piercing, as if it were looking into his soul. He found himself staring back, shivering against the brutal cold. The bird threw back its head, and a loud shriek escaped its narrow beak, echoing in the desolate woods. *Caw! Caw!*

"Oh, move your pathetic arse!" The voice behind him made him jump. It was loud and startled him. Before he could turn, he felt a boot connect with the small of his back, sending him stumbling forward into the snow. The air fled his lungs as he hit the ground, and he felt one of his ribs give away with a sickening 'snap'. He yelped and cried in pain as he lay there, his face buried in the snow like a beaten dog. His old bones rattled, and his breathing was reduced to a dry pant, each inhale pressing against the fresh fracture. He squinted against the fresh powder caked in his eyes and spit the dead leaves from his mouth with a pained whimper.

Behind him, the men cheered and laughed at his injury. They clinked their bottles and yelled more insults as he writhed in the snow, pausing only to erupt in cruel, drunken laughter.

"Pig-fucker!"

"Miserable Wretch!"

"Pathetic fool!"

Grundale could barely hear the words; the pain was starting to block out the noise. His head throbbed, and his lungs burned. He groaned in agony as his heart drummed in his chest. One of the men kicked at him, bruising his thighs repeatedly. Through the stomps, he felt a twinge of his own anger, and he found himself shouting at the men around him. Drool and slushed snow flicked from his lips as his voice struggled to hold together.

"Why?! What have I done to deserve such foul treatment? I am innocent!" Grundale's words were weak, defeated. His eyes welled with distraught fury. One of the men leaned in and responded with a boot, right between the eyes. As he went reeling, the man cursed and grabbed fistfuls of his coat, angrily yanking him to his feet like a child throwing a tantrum. He shouted in his face, and Grundale flinched against the slurred words. He couldn't really hear him. He was seeing doubles.

"We won't listen to your rot! We know you're guilty. The reverend told us so. He told us what you did to those kids. We ought to just kill you here. Maybe we should replicate the suffering you brought upon them. That will teach ya."

There were murmurs among the group, but nothing finite. The guard shoved him forward.

"Move!"

Grundale's legs shook, and he swayed as he tried to keep his balance. His feet were frozen, and his ears felt like they would shatter. With every hesitant step, he feared he would end up on the ground once more. His vision was blurred, and it felt like the forest was spinning around him.

When he didn't move, one of the townsmen drew a dagger from his belt and impatiently held it to his back. The steel was stiff and deadly, and he felt the shape of the blade through his coat. Grundale felt the man get close and speak, his stinking breath hot in his ear.

"I said move your bloody arse! Or I'll cut me a souvenir,"

The man brought the knife up and ran it across his own ear, mimicking a cutting sound. Grundale swallowed, the dry knot still residing in his throat. The man gave him a final shove, and after a few awkward steps, the old man pressed on.

Grundale Bloodletter was an innocent man. During his death march, he thought of the children's faces, the ones he was accused of harming. He remembered seeing them just a few days ago. They had turned up at his cottage, saying they were intent on playing in the woods and must've gotten lost in their adventures. Grundale offered to escort them back home, but they refused, assuring him that they knew the way.

After some reluctance, he let them go. But deep down, he felt like he should've helped them get home. He felt a burning guilt in his soul for letting them go unsupervised, and now he was paying the price. He understood the accusations and how it looked from their perspective. He was an easy suspect.

He remembered their faces, their names. He'd been saying them over and over in his head since the posse grabbed him in the middle of the night. The little boy was Jasper, and the little girl was Rosaline. Jasper and Rosaline. Son and daughter of Ulrich and Joseline. Their hair was curly and the color of straw, just like their parents'. He remembered their bouncing curls, bright and unique aside from the other children's hair. And their eyes, blue like a cloudless summer sky. Beautiful children, their whole lives ahead of them. *Murdered* by him, so they had said.

Grundale continued to limp on. It didn't matter what he thought now. His fate was already decided. Destined for execution. Nothing he could say would change the minds of the people. He was already dead, and they would take heart in witnessing his destruction. Through the dark trees, he could see the glow of torchlight in the distance, and above that, the looming figure of a grand cross. They were almost there.

Dawn was about to break as they reached the town. Ahead, Grundale could see flickering torches in the streets, hear the yammering of townspeople. He could sense the agitation, a feeling of unrest that seemed to reflect with the men behind him. They were angry, eagerly awaiting the arrival of the one responsible for their plight. Their murderer. Who could remember the last time the gallows had been used, or if they even still worked? Everything had been peaceful for so long.

Even behind the walls, he could see the massive structure of the church, dominating the small town at the end of the thoroughfare. It dwarfed the manors and shops built around it, painted in black and gold with a large stained-glass window in the front.

Behind him, the Watchmen quickened their pace. Their excitement was apparent, and as they mumbled amongst themselves, Grundale couldn't help but feel sick. They were ready for the spectacle; it was the reward for their long walk through the night. The old man's nose was running.

Crimson snot congealed on his upper lip as the wind hit his face. His uneven teeth chattered, and he shivered in his torn clothes, feeling as if the blood in his veins was slowing. His tired eyes were growing heavy, and his thin hair was left disheveled by the night gales. He could no longer feel the rope sawing at his wrists. His hands had gone numb.

The posse was met by an angry mob at the town's gate, in a flurry of violent disgust. Curses spat from people of all shapes and sizes, and projectiles hurtled from the dark in all directions. He couldn't believe the people he saw, people whose names he knew, hurrying over in their blind malice, vegetables and stones clutched in their hands. He swallowed and kept his head low, readying himself against the barrage. High above, the same crow flapped and perched on the church's cross, cawing maniacally once more.

When the horde of citizens hit, he winced at the assortment of shouts and curses loud in his aching ears. Men, women and children together, pushing and shoving to get their hands on his clothing. One lady slapped him across his face; another man landed a fist to his gut. Their insults were hurtful and horrible; every brand imaginable spat in his face as he was pushed through the angry masses.

"Monster!"

"Devil-Worshipper!"

"Child-killer!"

Grundale Bloodletter was an innocent man. He ignored their slander, and through gasping breaths, he again pleaded his own innocence. Tomatoes and rotten squash splattered against his shirt, and he looked down to see a young boy swatting him with a broken stick. They called him a demon, they called him a monster. One man shouted his name loudly, and he looked up in time to be struck by a thrown rock. He felt the skin over his brow split open and bleed.

A maddening dizziness washed over him, and he thought he would collapse, but the Watchmen shoved him onward. His tortured vision was an array of their tormenting faces, all shouting and spitting at him with all the energy they could muster. As it all rotated, he tossed his head to the side and retched with a sob, a mixture of blood and vomit at the feet of his assailants. He felt like his head was going to explode. His ears rang with the many voices that shrieked at him, nothing but screaming and pain and screaming and pain and—-

"Silence!"

After a sudden commanding voice, the shouting ceased. All fell silent, and the citizens slowly broke away, leaving Grundale standing alone, bleeding and gasping for breath. The spinning had stopped abruptly, and everything had come to a surreal sense of clarity. Then the old man looked up as the realization hit him. He was standing before the gallows, a single noose swaying high in the w ind.

Grundale stared at it for a moment before fresh tears leaked from his eyes, flowing over the previous dried tracks on his cheeks. He heard footsteps, a single pattern, approaching behind him. He turned slowly to see a tall man in a black robe, the collar and sleeves outlined with gold trim. Squinting through the blood dripping from his brow, he recognized him as the reverend, sole leader of their church, and by proxy, the town. He was known only as Letholdus, who swore himself as the vassal of their Almighty God. Many nodded respectfully as he approached, slow and confident. When he finally spoke to Grundale, it was as if this was nothing more than a friendly encounter.

"Well, Grundale, the time has come to pay for your sins. Will you accept your fate as a guilty man? Or take your lies to your grave, and be delivered into the fiery hands of hell?" He spoke elegantly, placing a gentle hand on his shoulder. The old man flinched at his touch, and when he spoke, his voice was cracked and weak.

"But... I'm... innocent. You know that."

Reverend Letholdus looked him in the eyes, and a sinister grin formed on his face.

"Very well. May our lord bestow mercy upon you." Letholdus turned on his heel and made some motion with his hand, and across the street he heard the clink of metal footsteps.

Grundale watched with contempt as three men, the reverend's personal guard, made their way towards him. Garbed in mail hauberks and plate armor, they moved like iron statues. Sheathed long swords bounced at their sides, with a bow and quiver strapped to each back. Their stares were cold and fierce—just the sight of them made the townspeople give them a wide berth.

Before Grundale could utter another word, two of the knights grabbed his arms, clamping down on his frail limbs with their bulky gauntlets. The third shoved passed him and ascended the staircase leading to the gallows, his greaves heavy with every step as he climbed the execution stage. Grundale's escorts yanked him up and forward, with such force that the toes of his shoes dragged helplessly underneath him. He could only obey weakly with his beaten limbs. They brought him up the stairs, every step more agonizing than the last. He shot looks at the crowd, hoping for someone to speak up for him, but out of all the faces gathered to see him, there wasn't a single one willing to pipe up.

A couple had pushed their way to the front of the surveying crowd. The man held his wife close, their blonde hair tossed by the wind. The woman was weeping, while the man wore a mask of pure hatred. Ulrich and Joseline had attended his execution. They wanted to see him hang for their children's anguish.

The church guard pulled him up the rest of the steps, ignoring his groans and whimpers. One of the armored men pulled a dagger and slit the ropes at his wrists, letting them fall to the wooden floor. He turned Grundale around and yanked off his fur coat, tossing it in the mud and leaving him in his loose shirt. They yanked his wrists behind his back and bound them again, tighter this time. Wincing against the painful restraints, he stood there helpless, the hungry eyes of the town leering up at him. Everyone was silent as he was readied; all he could do was shiver before them, his bare arms scrawled with goosebumps.

One of the knights fit the noose around his neck, while another made sure the rope was unflawed. The last manned the lever. The wind died down slightly, making way for a light snow. Grundale watched the sun rise in its many shades of pink and orange, the last sunrise he would ever see.

Above, the mischievous crow perched at the top of the gallows, on the mantle that held his noose. It cocked its head and cawed softly at him, almost sympathetically. The old man looked up at it, staring into its eyes that resembled little black marbles. The knight tightened the noose, holding the braid and pulling the rope until it choked him. Some citizens cheered, others threw more fruit and stones. Joseline stared at the ground while Ulrich kept his hateful stare. Reverend Letholdus maintained his grin.

Alas, the guards gave the signal that everything was prepared correctly. Letholdus gave a nod, and the old man heard the knight grasp the lever. He peeked at the ground through the cracks of the trap door, realizing how high above the ground he really was.

The audience waited, watching the knights with anticipation. Some looked excited, others ashamed. Some frowned upon him, while a few shared the same grin as the reverend. Others could barely mask their impatience.

The massive church bell rang, chiming loudly in the town square. Birds fluttered from nearby trees, startled by the noise. In the fluttering snow, Grundale counted the chimes, and rays of sunshine kissed his skin. Such a beautiful morning. Too beautiful for death.

"Wait!" said the old man, and the people jumped at his voice. The masses glanced at one another in surprise. The reverend stepped forward, raising his voice to the crowd.

"It appears our sinner has decided to speak!" he theatrically cast a hand to Grundale, "Tell me, Grundale Bloodletter, murderer and sadist of Jasper and Rosaline, do you beg for forgiveness in the eyes of our Lord?"

The townspeople hooted and booed him, shouting more names as he struggled to stand.

"Let him hang! Let him hang!" they chanted.

The old man waited for their anger to subside before speaking. He cleared his throat and made eye contact with as many as he could. Many perked up with interest.

"What have I done to deserve such an accusation? I have lived in this town for decades, and never have I lifted a finger against any woman or child." He paused to breathe, his lungs weak and gasping against his broken rib. Ulrich snarled, and Joseline looked up, her eyes puffy from weeping. Grundale looked at them directly as he continued.

"I have lived in my cottage for many a year, watching you children grow and mature into the people you are today. Never have I stolen, harmed, or cursed any of you. My days of war and violence are long behind me. I am a huntsman, and barely that in my old age. The loss of Jasper and Roseline pains me as much as any of you. I swear whatever has befallen them is not of my hand, nor of any of my kin. You are driven mad by their well-being, stringing up an innocent man in your desperation," The old man explained, shrugging as the wind accelerated and whipped at his clothes.

Letholdus clutched the decorated rosary around his neck, booming to the crowd.

"Blasphemy! This man speaks in place of the Devil! His tongue is turned wicked by the Dark One, and we shall purge the wicked with light!" The townspeople cheered, relishing in his words. Letholdus fed them more, jabbing a finger at the old man.

"You, Grundale Bloodletter, took the children and used their innocence for your own twisted desires. The Holy One sees *all* evil, and here you stand, trying to sway these good people with your silver tongue. We are immune to your lies, old man." The crowd grew louder.

The old man felt the amber ring on his pinky with his numb fingers. He fought back tears, feeling all was lost for him. When the townspeople died down, Grundale spoke again, trying to make his voice louder as he petitioned.

"I beg of you, please! Stop this madness. Your rage is making you blind. I am just an old man, not an instrument of death." He looked at Ulrich and Joseline, who just stood there amongst the chaos, "Please, know that I did not harm your children. My only regret is not escorting them home when I had the chance. I don't know what has befallen them, but I assure you I had nothing to do with it. *Free me.* I could help you find them, and we could put an end to this nonsense. Your hate will be your undoing. There is no going back from this," he urged them.

It was Joseline who spoke up first. She stared at him with accusing eyes, a mixture of hate and sadness.

"My daughter is gone. She will never bloom in life and grow old like you. How could you be so evil as to lie to our faces? She was just a girl, damn you!" she wailed and buried her face in Ulrich's chest. A single tear went down Ulrich's cheek, and he cleared his throat.

"My son will never make a family of his own. He will never feel the warmth of a woman or pass down his birthright. You're a monstrous slug, Grundale. We must stop you before you tear apart other families and cause more pain. If it weren't for my wife, I would wring your neck myself." Ulrich turned to the reverend, his sobbing wife in his arms.

"Let him hang."

The reverend held his rosary in the air for all to see.

"The people have decided your fate, old man. God help you." He ran a finger across his throat. The knights nodded and reached for the lever.

"No. You fools are the ones who need help," Grundale said, "you're all damned."

The knight yanked the lever home. With a shift of woodwork, the mechanisms released, and the door shot out from Grundale's feet. As he plummeted toward the earth, the rope stretched taut, and the old man's neck broke with a sickening snap. The crowd gasped at the terrible sound, and as he bounced on his rope, his eyes remained fixed on the people before him. His feet kicked inches above the ground in his final throes, and children cried as they hid from his perpetual stare. Men and women cringed at his twisting convulsions and bloodshot eyes, but they watched until the end. With a final gurgling breath, Grundale was no more, and the town returned the anguished glare of the fallen man with grim satisfaction. It wasn't until the reverend turned to them that they looked away. He cleared his throat and shouted to the people.

"The Devil's sentry has been vanquished! As he finds his way to hell, let us pray, and relish in the—"

The sound of the rope snapping interrupted him. It was loud and echoed through the thoroughfare like a cracked whip. The cord above the noose had broken in two, letting the old man's body fall to the ground. The corpse landed on its side, its eyes still holding a petrified gaze. In stunned silence, Letholdus and the townspeople stared back, holding their breath as they looked at the dead body. None of them could lift their eyes from him. The crow on the mantle threw its head back and cawed maniacally.

As everyone listened to the maddening cry, Grundale blinked.

Joseline and the other women screamed as the dead man opened his mouth to release a tortured groan. Grundale twitched and rolled onto his stomach, snow and dirt sticking to his face. He rose from the ground in a worming motion, inching his way up until he stood to face them. The knights cried in alarm, and the townspeople started to panic, recoiling in horror as they tried to flee, frantically bumping into one another.

Tremors shook the ground. With a loud gust of wind, a wall of fire rose from the earth, enveloping the walls of the town and consuming the main gate. The fire raged with contorted orange flames, circling around the church and the town square until it formed a perfect circle, trapping everyone in. Those who didn't jump back in time were consumed by the flames, burning their clothes and charring them to black skeletons in seconds with unexplainable heat. Reverend Letholdus cowered as the hellfire rose, calling to the knights for answers.

Grundale took a step towards the townspeople, his neck still bent at its grotesque angle. Behind him, the knights shouted amongst themselves and drew their bows, knocking arrows and taking aim. They opened fire at Grundale's back, but the arrows stopped inches from his flesh and dissolved into mists of ash. The old man's eyes rolled into the back of his head, showing nothing but veins and swollen membranes. With a jerk, he broke his neck back into place, rotating his head and stretching out the stiffness.

The knights continued to shoot; every arrow launched burning up into nothing. The old man balled his bound hands into fists, straining against the entwined rope. His amber ring emitted a dull glow, the dark red gemstone at the center sparkling red hot. Grundale's appearance began to change; his freckled, wrinkled skin smoothed, and his thin hair shed from his scalp, making way for a new mane, long and black like the crow's feathers. It grew until it cascaded down his back, shiny locks blowing in the erratic wind. He hunched over, his face hidden under the hair. The dead old man shook violently, and his veins pulsed and popped like straw. His skin stretched as newly toned muscle bulged within. The ragged loose shirt was now filled with a broad chest and square shoulders, the trousers accompanied by lean legs. The noose was stretched tight across his neck.

The reverend watched in disbelief, unable to look away from the dead man's transformation. The townspeople scrambled about, pointing and screaming at the charred corpses that lay smoking at the edge of the thoroughfare. Letholdus pointed a finger at the large cross and shouted over the chaos.

"The church! Get to the church! It will protect us from the monster's wrath!!"

They nodded and flocked to the divine structure, knocking into one another while they clung to their loved ones. Letholdus looked back at Grundale and saw a man fifty years younger. He looked nothing like the one they had just executed. He moved slowly at first, joints cracking as he took awkward steps towards him.

Down the street, the townsfolk arrived at the church. Leading the group was one of the Watchmen, still holding his torch in his gloved hand. He shoved the large double doors of the church open and started waving people into the pews. Before anyone could go in, the doors slammed shut, crushing the Watchman's arm like a wooden bite. The townspeople screamed in terror as he withdrew a bloody stump.

"Dear God," whispered the reverend, his gaze locked with the man who was once Grundale Bloodletter. He returned his gaze with a glowing stare, his eyes red as roses. The rope binding his wrists shimmered and turned to serpents. They hissed and slithered away, burrowing into the frozen earth like worms. The cawing crow flapped from the mantle and landed on the man's shoulder, cocking its head while it looked at the reverend. The young man rubbed his wrists; the chafed skin had healed completely. He looked at the church, narrowing his sinister eyes as he watched the scared townsfolk get ready to break the windows. The reverend followed his gaze. Another Watchmen picked up a rock and hefted it over his head, ready to smash the window. Before he could swing, the window exploded outward, sending a hail of glass into his eyes and face. Other shards sliced the men and women around him, and they wailed in agony as the glass buried deep within their skin.

The young man watched with an emotionless expression. Behind him, one of the Knights drew his sword, rushing at him with the blade raised.

"Die, you demon!!"

He brought the blade down with a battle cry, aiming for the young man's neck. The blade burst into dozens of angry crows mid-swing, ones that immediately shrieked and swarmed the knight. They pecked around his armor and tore strips of flesh from the openings, pecking incessantly with their bloody beaks. He tried to swat at them, but there were too many, the black blur swirling around. In seconds, the knight stumbled into the snow, his armor a bloody mess, his eyes plucked from their sockets.

From the gallows, the remaining two knights continued to rain arrows down upon him to no avail. The young man waved a hand in annoyance, and a hot flash of light burst from the open trap door. Their armor and chainmail melted, pools of molten metal pouring down their bodies. Muscle fell away from bone in seconds. Their screams were cut short by their liquified suits, and the crow cried mockingly as they were reduced to gooey piles of flesh.

The birds stormed the skies. They attacked all who had cheered for the execution. As they ran for their lives, wicked earthen hands sprouted from the ground and pulled some into the broken soil like quicksand. Men and women thrashed and fought to free themselves, but the summoned hands were much stronger, bruising flesh and breaking bones as they were forced to have their lungs filled with dirt. Their cries faded as they were pulled deeper and deeper underground until nothing remained of their demise but a solidifying frozen crust.

The reverend cried as the elements slaughtered them. He could only watch the destruction. As the Young man drew close to him, he shouted a prayer, but it only blended in with the chaos around him. He continued to chant, holding the rosary out in defense as the monster before him advanced. The amber ring continued to glow, swirling colors of red and violet vacating the stone embedded in the band. The noose around the Young Man's neck loosened and floated off him, hanging between the two of them in an uncanny stillness. Tears welled in the reverend's eyes as he stared at it, his face a pained grimace as everything he knew, everything he understood, shattered before him. The levitated noose gravitated towards the reverend slowly, and when he turned to run, it shot towards his neck and tightened fiercely. The frayed lead lifted him off the ground, suspending him in the air just as the old man had been, just moments before. He coughed and clawed at the sentient rope, but it only squeezed tighter, burying into his skin as he thrashed in th e air.

Thick black smoke billowed from the windows of the church, and a fire raged within. No one had witnessed the start of it, but now eager tongues of flame spewed from the broken windows. The crow on the young man's shoulder stared at the convulsing Letholdus, the fire's glow dancing in its beady eyes. The young man raised his hand, and the ground quaked, leaving the remaining civilians stumbling for safety. Behind the floating reverend, there was the sound of creaking lumber, and the church's foundation separated as it was ripped from the ground. The burning church hurtled into the sky, raining death in the form of broken boards and smoldering pews. The debris fell with loud crashes, burying those below like falling meteors. The reverend watched with bulging eyes as the flaming church crumbled to nothing, and the town's populace was reduced to stragglers. The grand cross was the last to fall, and as it came tumbling down, the rope tightened until his neck gave way, just as Grundale's had.

As the last of the fiery hell fell, the crows continued to swarm. Those who could not escape the murder found salvation in the roaring flames. The children, unharmed as they were, hugged themselves on the ground, weeping. And with the wave of the young man's hand, the slaughter stopped as suddenly as it started. The crows flew away, leaving corpses of those eaten alive behind them. Flames snuffed immediately, leaving nothing but piles of blackened bones. Smoke billowed from the charred earth as all the supernatural limbs retreated into the ground, as if they never existed. The torched scars in the earth and the bodies of those littering the thoroughfare served as reminders of the onslaught, steaming and twitching in the winter air. The reverend's lifeless body fell to the ground, joining all the others who had hurt the old man only moments before.

The young man stood amongst the wreckage like a ghost. Without any word or gesture, he walked through the wreckage to the now clear main gate. His steps were gentle, soundless. He stepped over rubble, charred cadavers, severed limbs. Those left alive cried softly and crawled away from him, and the crow mocked them loudly. He was almost at the end of the square when someone spoke to him.

"Wait," the voice was a man's, deeply pained and afraid.

The young man and the crow turned to see Ulrich, sitting against one of the many houses. In his arms was his wife, Joseline, lifeless and still. A large shard of stained glass was buried in her throat. He looked up at him, his hate washed away by fear. He wiped at his eyes before speaking again.

"What are you?" he asked.

The survivors watched him for a time, each with their own petrified stare.

"I am the voice of the innocent." His voice was a multitude of voices combined, all speaking together in a chorus of power. Ulrich looked down at his deceased wife, then at the bodies around him.

"Why? Why have you done this?"

"I only did what had to be done. In your hate and selfishness, you put an innocent man to death. A man who only wanted to help," the being said, his amber ring glinting in the rising sun.

Ulrich shook his head angrily, "Grundale Bloodletter took and butchered my children! We only wanted justice."

"No. You wanted death. And the church granted it, using your ignorance and grief against you. You didn't even think to ask *why*," They spoke.

"But the reverend said—" Ulrich stammered, but was cut off.

"The reverend fed you lies. Your children were never slain, human. They've been here all along. Grundale tried to tell you, but instead you spat in his face and *silenced* him."

Ulrich sobbed. "Where? Where are my children?"

The being stared for a moment. Then, without looking, he pointed at the cathedral, to the crater it left behind.

"Deep under the church, there's a hidden cellar. They're in there, unharmed. Where they've been the whole time, they were to be sacrificed in the name of your Almighty God. The reverend knew he could make you see his way. He needed a way to explain the children's disappearance. I warned Grundale before you took him from his home. I told him of their plans to kill him as a scapegoat to give you closure. I gave him the choice to flee, but he refused, thinking he could make you see the truth. But you didn't. He was foolish, but a good man. He believed he could make you see reason. When he knew all was lost, he granted me his body as a vassal of retribution. You all brought this upon yourself. The answers were there; all you had to do was *listen*."

The being walked on, leaving Ulrich amongst the wreckage. He looked at his wife, then to the crater left behind by the destroyed church. As the young man left, Ulrich called to him a final time.

"What do we do now? How do we move on from this? I don't know what to do."

The being considered it for a moment, and spoke as it walked away.

"Learn from your mistakes."

FOREVER AND ALWAYS

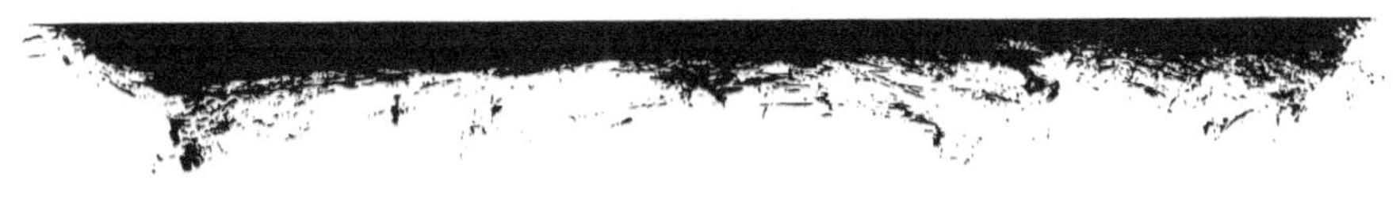

For the seventh time, Meryl's call went to voicemail. With a sigh, she hung up, staring hopelessly at her husband's contact photo. Head to toe in camo, he stared back with a toothy smile, one she wished more than anything she could see right now.

Hours ago, Wesley had a doctor's appointment, one she had scheduled herself. It was just supposed to be a courtesy checkup following a tumble he took on his four-wheeler that morning, mostly an excuse for him to get his yearly visit out of the way.

Now it was nearly 10 pm, and Wesley had not returned home. Not as much as a call or text since he had arrived there. She knew his family doctor was notorious for taking forever, but she couldn't imagine why she hadn't gotten a single message explaining why he hadn't returned home. Any other time, he'd answer, whether he was in the truck or at the pharmacy. This was unlike him. He always checked in if something took longer than usual.

Unless there's something wrong, she thought incessantly.

When her mind flashed back to his wreck on the ATV—the handlebars under his jaw so tight she thought he'd broken his neck—she couldn't help but shiver. Luckily, the log he was pinned against was mostly dead and had some give to it. Even still, she couldn't help but fear the worst.

Meryl paced the kitchen in frustration. It didn't make any sense. She was on the HIPAA forms; if they found something and he needed to be transferred, they would've called her. If he were stuck at the pharmacy waiting on a prescription, he would've let her know. His phone wasn't dead—it rang and rang until it hit voicemail. She had even tried the doctor's office and had gotten the same results. A bunch of ringing with no answers. She was plagued by thoughts of a disaster of some kind unfolding, and the phones just uselessly ringing in the background. Her world could be on fire, and she wouldn't have a clue. All she knew was he had made it there.

In the living room, their old grandfather clock ticked with every tick, reminding her of every passing second. It seemed to grate on her nerves, but she supposed it was better than dead silence.

Tick... tock... tick... tock the pendulum swung.

She had heard of people mistaking whiplash for a broken neck. They would've, *should've* called her if it was something drastic. What if he were concussed and got into an accident on the way home? How soon would be *too soon* to report him missing? Should she be calling the police?

Meryl looked over his last text on her phone, the message haunting her.

-I just signed in. They have The Lion King this time. Happy now?-

She set it on the counter and tried to hold back tears.

Through their years of marriage, Wesley had often called her a worrywart. He had a reputation for living recklessly, between the ATVs and the guns. Somehow, whenever things got hairy, he always managed to emerge unscathed and smiling. As much as she wanted to pretend this was one of those times, she couldn't ignore the welling pit in her stomach.

Through the front window, a light caught her attention. A pair of headlights swung into the driveway. He was home.

Oh, thank god.

She eagerly waited by the window, thankful he had turned up. But the longer she looked, the more her relief began to fade. The headlights were different, and the vehicle was too low to the ground. It wasn't Wesley's truck that had pulled in. It was a police officer's.

Meryl's heart sank, and she braced herself for the worst. The squad car slowed to a stop, and a uniformed man emerged. She watched him from the window, a slow, almost practiced stroll as he made his way to the porch and into the dark.

A heavy knock rattled the front door. The sound was angry, like someone had pounded with the bottom of their fist. Meryl left the kitchen and nervously approached the door, feeling the crawl of goosebumps when she saw the silhouette standing on the other side in the dark.

She swallowed her unease and flicked on the porch light. The man didn't move at all, just stood there with his arms at his sides. His black uniform was decorated in stripes and a badge, a pair of sunglasses blocking his eyes. Several trickles of sweat on his forehead reflected the porch light above. He seemed oblivious to her standing there, watching.

"Coming," she said, mostly to urge herself on. She was trying not to panic, but his presence only solidified how dire the situation felt. She thought that if she didn't answer the door, it didn't have to be *real.* She wished she could just ignore him and run into her bedroom, hide under the covers. Instead, she felt herself stiffen and head to the front door.

Meryl took a deep breath before cracking it. The police officer turned his head to face her, another trickle of sweat running down his temple and onto his jacket. Despite his build, he looked physically sick, like the color had been drained from him.

"Can I help you?" she asked, looking up at the officer. He said nothing for a moment, chewing the inside of his cheek before curling it into a forced smile. He cleared his throat and started to speak.

"Good evening, ma'am. I'm with the Dyer Falls Police Department. I have some questions regarding your husband. May I come in?"

His words were strange. They sounded rehearsed, but lacking the authority she expected an officer to have.

"What's this about? Is something wrong?" Meryl asked, a sickening knot forming in her stomach. She opened the door a little more, but kept it between them as she looked behind him.

His squad car was parked further down the driveway. It appeared to be still running, but the headlights were off.

"When's the last time you saw your husband, ma'am? Have you heard from him recently?" He inquired, another bead of sweat rolling down his head.

"Did something happen to him? Is he alright?" Meryl demanded.

"We're trying to figure that out, ma'am. Is he home now? Can I speak with him, please?" the officer said, stepping toward the door. Meryl didn't open it further.

They don't even know where he is. So he hasn't been arrested.

"He's not home. He had a doctor's appointment, and he hasn't returned yet. I haven't heard from him," Meryl said, looking past the officer to the squad car. Someone was sitting in the passenger seat, their clothing unusually bright.

"Do you have any idea where he might be? It appears... there's been an accident," The officer said, after some hesitation.

"What kind of accident? Is he okay? What happened?" Meryl pleaded, feeling the welling of tears in her eyes. Her grip on the knob started to soften, and her legs suddenly felt weak. She felt like she was going to faint.

"We're not entirely sure. We're still trying to piece everything together. Can I come in? I have some questions I need to ask you," The officer explained, but Meryl only half heard him.

Her head started to swim, the whirlwind of mental scenarios acting up again as she thought of the tumbling four-wheeler. What could the police possibly want with him?

She looked at the officer again. His sunglasses, the sweat, the lack of headlights. His passenger. Something didn't feel right.

"You can ask your questions from there, thank you," she stated, holding the door firm.

The cop twitched and licked his lips.

"Surely there wouldn't be a problem with letting me in? I'm a police officer," he said aloud, like he was addressing a classroom. But he didn't make any gestures with his hands when he spoke; he just stood there straight, ominously. Another drop of sweat dampened his uniform.

"I can see that. But I'm not letting you in unless you have a warrant. What is this about? What do you mean by *accident*? Why do you need to see my husband? And who's that hanging out in your car?" Meryl pointed a finger, standing straighter.

"Warrant?" he repeated, confused. From behind his sunglasses, it was impossible to read him.

"Yeah. I'm not exactly sure what you're doing here," Meryl said, thinking quickly, "and if you want to come in, you're gonna need a warrant. Have you been drinking on the job? What's your badge number?"

She imagined the questions would provoke some anger, if anything. Whatever this was, it didn't feel right, and she was hoping it would scare him off. But he remained standing there and tilted his head slowly.

"I just need to speak to your husband, Meryl," he said coldly.

"How do you know my name?"

The officer turned his upper body towards the squad car as if he was side-eyeing it. The passenger door promptly opened, and a man stepped out. He was dressed like a construction worker, his reflective vest glowing in the porchlight. He was even wearing a hard hat.

While the officer was turned, she could see a swelling on the back of his neck. It looked like an inflamed sore of some kind, but something was protruding from it, like a thorn.

What the fuck?

"Don't make this harder than it has to be," he warned, turning back to her. He reached up and scratched at the spot on his neck, like he was agitated.

"We're done here," Meryl said, "I'm going to call the station. Next time, bring a warrant." She closed the door, and she felt sick when it stopped in its place. The man had jammed it with his boot and started leaning forward. She tried to shove it closed, but it wouldn't move.

"We're not leaving until we see your husband," he said plainly.

"Who's we? Get the fuck off my property! *Now!*" Meryl commanded, raising her voice.

None of it made sense. The officer's animosity put her off. She lived out in the country, where people had bonfires, drank beer, and shot off guns—never had the police come out, even when things got rowdy. Meryl didn't understand why Wesley hadn't come home or at least called. She didn't understand why this shady "police officer" was standing on her doorstep. Least of all, she didn't understand why the man with the hard hat and sunken eyes was flanking around the house, with a sledgehammer in his hand.

Meryl looked at the officer to see him smiling. He reached in quickly, grabbing for her shirt. With all her might, she threw herself against the door and watched it clamp down on his arm. He groaned in anger and shouldered into it, nearly knocking her off her feet. Her mind raced. The back door was locked, the garage door was locked, if she could get to her phone—

The door flew open, sending her staggering. Meryl bolted for the kitchen, made eye contact with the phone, just in time to feel two hands shove her hard. She hit the ground a second later and immediately rolled to face her attacker, but he wasn't coming right after her.

The officer grabbed her smartphone from the counter and looked at it curiously, before slowly looking down at her. As she climbed to her feet, the officer held the phone in both hands and snapped it in half, without as much as a grimace.

Terrified, Meryl opened the utensil drawer and felt for something to defend herself—a knife, a fork, anything. The officer charged her again, and she yanked the drawer from its track in a panic, swinging the whole thing at once. The officer took it on the chin with a meaty *smack,* utensils showering the entire kitchen. His chin split and started to bleed, but it only seemed to annoy him. She swung it again, and he swatted it away so hard it twisted out of her hands. The drawer clattered to the floor, and his arms found her collar, clammy hands snatching fistfuls of her blouse before he quickly slammed her into the stove. He pushed against her with such force that it shattered the glass of the oven's door. She yelped as her shoulders screamed with pain, pixelated remains of the tempered glass showered the floor. Screaming while she tried to twist out of his grip, the fabric of her blouse tore, and she raked at his face in retaliation, knocking the sunglasses to the floor.

His eyes were menacing, bloodshot. Like they were about to burst from their sockets, he fought with her clumsily, but he was strong, overpowering her with ease. He smelled of sweat and *dirt,* a permeating stench that wafted with him like a cloud, like he had been rolling around in mud. Between the insanity of the attack, his appearance, and the thought that there was *another* man with him lurking somewhere, Meryl was only certain of one thing: these men showed up intending to hurt her as well as her husband. Since he wasn't home, there was no telling what they planned to do.

"Let me go—get the fuck away from me!" she cried, doing everything she could to get him to let her go. She slapped and clawed, punched him in the nose. When she got a proper footing, she drove a knee between his legs. He faltered for a moment and let go, only to clamp his hands around her neck instead. They stumbled, and she hit the ground hard, landing awkwardly on the scattered utensils and bits of glass as the cop came crashing down on top of her. Immediately, she felt the oppressive weight of him, along with the squeeze of his cold fingers around her throat. It was clear he was done playing around, and she felt like he would crush her windpipe if he squeezed any harder. She reached for his face, aiming for his eyes, and instead found the damp meat of his cheek.

Meryl didn't care where she dug her fingers, as long as it hurt. As she felt the iron grip tighten around her throat, she shoved her thumb into his cheek, hooking her fingers under his jaw. His skin was cold and slick, but it gave under her fingertips as she desperately latched on to him. She wanted to hurt him enough to let her go, but he didn't as much as make a sound of discomfort as she felt a tooth *give* under the weight of her thumb. His jaw parted slightly, giving her something to hold on to as she pulled as hard as she could. It wasn't until she felt the sickening *pop* against her fingers that she looked to see what was happening.

Her first thought was of a stroke, the way his face sagged. But when she felt the rush of blood over her knuckles and onto her blouse, her mind started to comprehend what was transpiring. With a sickening tear, his face was *coming off.*

"Oh god!" Meryl screamed, the skin suddenly feeling like putty in her hand.

Beginning at his temple, it tore away as a continuous strip—an inch-thick slab of muscle, teeth, and gelatinous bone. The officer didn't flinch, didn't breathe as the tear continued under his nose, holding the same menacing glare as she looked in horror at what was left in its wake.

Lurking beneath the strands of remaining gore was a hardened faceplate, chittering mandibles where his mouth used to be. It was like something was wearing him. Like a suit.

Meryl recoiled and let the flesh go in fear. The flap dangled and dripped, the inside of nicotine-stained molars and stark white jawbone hanging like pieces of a discarded mask. He leaned closer to her, the flap nearly touching her as his eyes unfocused and drifted. It was like they had powered off. His body began to vibrate, and deep within his chest, she heard the sounds of snakes slithering through meat.

Outside, there was a loud crunch, the sound of metal on metal. The "officer" holding her down released a hand and drew it back, the attached wrist bending back unnaturally until it broke with the sickening sound of snapping twigs. A barb worked its way through the flesh of the break, a wicked hook that serrated the skin as it emerged, curving out of the forearm like a sickle made of dark bone.

Meryl reached blindly for a weapon, sticky digits leaving streaks on things that couldn't help her. Rubber tongs—ladle—plastic spatula. Just as she felt her fingers curl around the familiar wooden T of the corkscrew, the power blinked out, drowning them both in darkness.

Meryl thrust the corkscrew so hard it jarred her wrist. The grip released and thrashed about, a metallic shriek erupting in the dark. She could see it faintly in the moonlight, angry and confused, a glimmer of the utensil sticking out from its head. Wherever she had gotten him, it hurt. Gasping for breath, she shoved it off and disappeared into the dark, hurrying away from it as far and fast as she could.

She coughed and gasped for breath as she fought to keep from stumbling. Behind her, she heard the sounds of cabinets breaking, dishes shattering. Meryl didn't waste any time. With her phone gone and keys lost to the dark, she only knew one thing that would give her any kind of chance.

Upstairs was their bedroom. And in the bedroom, there was the gun safe.

In the darkness, the clock ticked, as if timing her.

Tick... tock... tick... tock.

Through the impetuous black, Meryl felt for the handrail of the stairs and ascended, paddling up the carpeted steps. She hoped she'd have a minute before they realized where she was going—hoped she'd at least have enough time to lock the door behind her. She didn't think it would keep them out, but hoped it would buy her precious seconds. The generator had a startup time of two minutes—as long as they weren't heading for it next. This thought and more raced through her head as she entered their bedroom, shut the door behind her, and locked it.

She had only backed away for a second before rushing over and shoving her shoulder against a nearby dresser, a despairing attempt at barricading the door. Once that was done, she hurried over to the safe and squinted at the keypad in the dark. There wasn't enough light in the room to see the numbers, and she hoped she'd still be able to get into it. Wesley would know, he would have a plan, he would have the *keys.* She knew there was a spare set, but she was mentally kicking herself because she couldn't remember where they were. She never thought she'd see the day when she'd have to open the damn thing, let alone in the dark.

Boy, was she wrong.

Luckily, the keypad was battery-operated and lit up at first touch. She *did* know the code. Her first attempt was a failure, as she went too quickly and her thumb slipped on the last digit. The second was a success—a well-memorized anniversary date—and she was rewarded with a rapid green flash. She pulled the heavy steel handle, and its large deadbolts retracted, letting it swing open slowly.

She only knew how to use one of the firearms comfortably, and she groped blindly until she felt its familiar double tube. She pulled it from the rack, the weight of it making her anxious. She set on finding shells next, crouching behind the shield of the safe's door as she fumbled with boxes. She knew what she'd need, but didn't exactly know where it was. She clumsily tore open one box and immediately felt the spill of too small, too hard bullets. She needed *shells,* not bullets.

Fuck. Fuck!

She dropped them in the safe and picked the next mystery box, one that felt closer to what she needed, but found the shells within to be too skinny. She mumbled to herself as she urged herself on, trying and mostly failing not to panic.

"I don't need 4-10, I need twelve," she whispered to herself, feeling the fleet of time in her struggle. The next box was bigger, bulkier—a near-perfect square. She ripped open the lid and found solace in the fat, plastic cartridges with flanged ends within. They had to be them. The box slipped from her slick palms and spilled onto the floor, but not before she was able to grab two of them.

Meryl broke open the over and under 12-gauge shotgun and repeated the motions she had done countless times on clay pigeon shootings. The rounds slid in with a *thunk, thunk,* and she snapped it closed, cradling it in her arms as she looked towards the bed, a good spot for cover and bracing herself.

Before she left the safe, she saw the faint outline of her husband's ear muffs hanging near the top. They were electronic hearing protectors, one of the greatest inventions for wives who got drug along to range days. She swiped them before scurrying around the bed, minding the shotgun's long length.

Meryl pulled the muffs over her ears and hunkered down with the gun before reaching up and turning them on. When the surrounding sound hit her muffled ears, she felt her heart race. She could hear more than she thought she would, an amount that was helpful, but nearly overwhelming. In the dark and quiet house, she could hear *everything.*

Downstairs, she could hear the officer, or whatever it was, pacing the living room. His footsteps were heavy, and she could faintly hear the floorboards creak with every step. She could hear the incessant tick of the grandfather clock. She could hear the wind against the house. It was like an audio program of her own home invasion.

Without warning, the grandfather clock began to chime, signaling the top of the hour. *Ten o'clock.* It spun up loudly like it always did, a *clang-clang-clang* that would constantly agitate her when she was in the room with it. The footsteps stopped for a moment, only for them to speed up suddenly like they were crossing the room in angry strides. The clock whined as it was smashed to pieces, so hard it rattled the walls in the house. The tantrum didn't stop until she heard it get tossed around the room, where the house fell eerily quiet again. The footsteps resumed almost immediately.

Meryl tightened her grip on the gun and waited. She heard the intruder stop at the landing, like they were at the bottom of the stairs, looking up. They took them two at a time, methodically climbing with creaks that got louder the closer they got. Meryl wasn't sure if they were trying to sneak or keep from falling. The steps continued until they met the carpet outside her door, where they stood for a moment, as if considering. If they had a gun, would they be able to shoot her first?

Come on.

Meryl always wondered whether she'd have the gumption to shoot a man in their house, and always teetered on the assumption that Wesley would manfully handle it himself. But he wasn't here, and whatever that thing was outside her door, it definitely was no man. Not anymore, at least. Now, as she tried and steadied her breathing, she was more worried about pulling the trigger too soon. She didn't want to miss—she didn't think she'd be getting the time to reload if she did.

She heard them try the knob first, a firm wiggle that let them know the door was locked. It seemed to growl in annoyance, a metallic trill that gave her the chills in the surround sound. The next noise was so loud it startled her. The officer threw himself into the door so hard that pictures fell from the walls. The door held at first, but on the second time she heard the wood splinter. Each consecutive ram was more difficult than the last, and she could quickly hear the wood and hinges surrendering.

Meryl flicked off the safety and rested her finger on the trigger. Her heart thundered in her chest. Ahead, as her eyes adjusted, she saw the shift of the door as it broke from its hinges, the blur of shadows as it slammed into the dresser. It rocked wildly in protest.

Meryl held the gun as tight as she could against her shoulder to try and keep it from shaking. A screech echoed in the hall.

The door exploded inward, and the dresser toppled over. Meryl lined the bead with the center of the figure in the doorway and squeezed both triggers.

BOOM-BOOM!

The muzzle flash was bright and only showed the horror for a second, right before both barrels emptied into it. The recoil knocked her on her ass, hitting the bedside wall behind her in a daze. After the muffling of the headphones, she heard the aftermath of the shots hit their mark—the body stumbling back and crumbling down the steps with the sounds of clubbed meat and breaking bones. She listened to it roll to a stop at the bottom of the landing and cease movement.

The generator roared to life, and the power flicked on. Meryl winced against the light but didn't shift her gaze from the doorway, listening intently and staring into the dim stairwell. Even as she thumbed the lever on the gun and ejected the shells. Smoke danced and tickled her nostrils, and she sat there for a moment, lost in the fact that she had fired off the gun in their home.

A second later, she threw up. She had shot a man. Probably killed him.

Wesley would be proud of that shot, she thought bitterly, before wiping her mouth and picking herself up. With no more noises to be heard, she moved to the front of the gun safe, where the array of ammunition littered the floor. She plucked more shells from the carpet, little maroon cartridges acting as her only assurance in the silence. She reloaded quickly and snapped the gun shut once more, before grabbing as many as she could hold in her hand. Her pockets were small and not accommodating to shotgun shells, but she was able to cram five until the denim bulged at max capacity. Just as she was gathering more to fill her other pocket, the headphones picked up something that made her freeze in place.

It was buzzing, a vibration of sound that made her feel as though a fly was hovering around her ear. She looked around, confused, unable to place anything in the house that would produce such a noise. It got louder and louder until the sound was unbearable in her ears.

It was coming from outside.

Meryl dreadfully looked at the bedroom window, just in time to stifle a scream. The glass exploded inward as the construction worker impossibly shoved his head through, his hard hat acting as a battering ram. Meryl fumbled with the gun as she crawled backwards, moving away from the man who now gripped the sill, ignoring the glass that cut into his palms. The buzzing got so loud that the headphones cut out.

There was no life behind his eyes, no color in his face. He looked more stricken than the officer, like his skin barely clung to his bones. As he tried to pull himself in, his body made a retching motion, like he was trying to vomit. On the fourth heave, a stinger burst from his mouth, the tip vibrating so fast she felt a tingling sensation in the air, on her *skin*. It hummed like an industrial drill—just looking at the thing filled Meryl with a dread unlike anything she'd ever felt before. She couldn't help but think of it piercing her skull, rooting around before blending the soft tissues of her brain.

The mass continued to work its way out of him, bulging his throat and widening his jaw until it dislocated, the skin splitting to accommodate what looked like a growing, bulbous abdomen.

Meryl had seen enough. She pulled the trigger before she could even think to look down the barrel. The first cluster missed for the most part, exploding the skin between his bleeding hands. The second, however, hit him square in the face.

In an explosion of red and industrial plastic, the man slipped from the window, leaving nothing behind but a pair of bloody fingerprints. Meryl heard the buzzing fade away, and she picked herself off the floor a second time.

This is insanity, what the fuck, Meryl mentally screamed as she grabbed the barrel firmly and thumbed the lever. The ejected shells tumbled away, and a shaking hand dug two more from her pocket. The receiver was warm to the touch and accepted the cartridges through a trickle of smoke. She needed to find her keys, get out of there and find help. *Actual* police. But could she trust them?

As Meryl toiled with the thought, she felt her stomach drop. She could hear the buzzing. It was getting louder again, but this time it was faster. It was rocketing toward the house, angrily. She snapped the gun shut and trained it on the broken window, waiting for a clear shot.

She wouldn't get one.

To the left of the window, the wall erupted like a bomb had gone off. Meryl could only catch a glimpse of it as it plowed through the rubble—a combination of twisted limbs and wings that flew so fast it soared over the bed and crashed into the master bathroom. Drywall and broken studs showered the bed and floor in the aftermath, and she could hear the monster thrashing about, shattering the toilet, the vanity. Meryl considered closing the bathroom door, but a primal realization overcame her.

Even with the shotgun, she was out of her depth. She needed to run.

Meryl fled the bedroom, side-stepping the toppled dresser and broken door. Shotgun aimed, she worked her way down the stairs, thankful for the lights provided by the generator. She paused halfway down the flight, her eyes fixing on the red stain that coated the bottom steps to the landing. It wasn't the blood that worried her—she had expected that. It was what wasn't there, what she was sure she would have to step over. Where she had expected to find a body, she found nothing but ruined carpet and shreds of black clothing.

The police officer was gone.

Go, just go—Meryl urged, reluctantly stepping over it. If she could just get her keys, she could get the fuck out of there. She could hear the thing upstairs, the buzzing of wings navigating debris as it looked for her. She wouldn't have much time. But if she hurried, maybe she could drive fast enough to outrun it.

When she rounded the corner into the kitchen, she couldn't aim the gun fast enough. Before she could even comprehend the struggle, it was over—one lightning-quick movement knocked the gun from her hand, before she felt the merciless grip of *claws* around her throat. A single arm hefted her towards the ceiling, higher and higher until the back of her neck was pressed painfully into the stucco.

The officer had her, and he had *changed.*

What was left of his face leered at her angrily, a storm of contempt brewing behind its single remaining eye. The other half of its face was alien to her, flat and smooth as stone, with a color that reminded her of the ripe cucumber. The corkscrew had been pulled free from what looked like a large, hex-patterned eye. It bled a dark green and looked like it was on the verge of deflating.

But it wasn't the still-hanging flap of face that scared her—it was what she saw below. The eye and the black officer's shirt were all that was left of its humanity. Withering gore and fabric lay in a bloody pile on the floor, like it had molted from the waist down. With the flesh discarded, it stood imposingly with the legs of a grasshopper, each bent backwards and covered in thorns.

I'm going to die from bug people, Meryl thought ludicrously. As she grasped at her throat, her only comfort was that her husband wasn't home, and he was safe from whatever this madness was. She hoped he would be okay, wherever he was.

The headphone's muffling crumbled against the shriek that escaped its maw, an excited cry so loud it rattled her bones. Before she knew it, she was tumbling through the living room, thrown with such force that the world spun as the floor battered her limbs, the headset flying off in the process. Her head knocked, and her joints cried. She rolled to a stop next to the coffee table, and as she gasped for breath again, she started to crawl under it for protection.

The grasshopper sang. Its footsteps followed quickly, three rapid strides before it upended the coffee table with one quick motion, sending it crashing into the wall. It kicked her over to face it, a single three-pronged foot holding her in place while it looked down on her. As it tilted its head in amusement, a set of bloody antennae pierced through the human scalp, long and twitching.

Behind it, the other invader made its way down the stairs. It walked on the contorted remains of its human hands, the head brutally ripped in two, stretched over the base of the menacing stinger. The top half of it was a mangled mess—the denimed legs ripped away and the pelvis eviscerated in the wake of a teardrop-shaped head with black, soulless eyes. Wings buffeted behind it faster than the human eye could see, buzzing so loud it shook the walls around it. A wasp abomination, wearing a man in the worst way. It joined its companion and looked down on her, the black eyes portraying nothing but pure, malicious hate. Between its "legs", its stinger probed the air hungrily.

They didn't ask for last words or offer any kind of remorse. Meryl watched the grasshopper lift its foot from her chest and position it over her head, the realization of the end dangling like a guillotine. She didn't have the energy to try and avoid it. If she didn't roll, it would surely break her arms. It flexed its toes in preparation for the stomp, and Meryl wondered if it would hurt or if she would simply cease to think.

She closed her eyes. She didn't want to see it coming.

The commotion to follow sounded like a car had crashed through the front of the house. A chorus of demonic screeching resonated in the air—two in fear and one of unbridled hate—and she felt a gust of wind wash over her, right before it crashed into the opposite wall.

Meryl opened her eyes. The window she had peeked out of when the officer arrived just moments ago was gone, as was the majority of the wall surrounding it. Something had come through it, something *bigger* than the wasp. She heard shrieks and the scratch of legs against the hardwood, and her eyes widened at the scene taking place.

Even hunched, it loomed over the grasshopper. The wasp backed away with an unmistakable look of fear, retreating towards the kitchen while the grasshopper was overpowered into the wall, its hind legs kicking as it was lifted off its feet. A new, third atrocity was staring it in the face, pinning it against the wall, its arms curved like serrated scythes. The legs arched from its long torso, allowing it to easily dominate the grasshopper even as it tried to shove it off.

Wings stained in blood, massive eyes filled with rage. It looked like a praying mantis from another world. And it was pissed.

It was over in an instant. The serrated arms ripped down in a cross cut, reducing the monster that had tormented her into three pieces, separating it from the neck and waistline. Its life twinged away in gushes of dark green, its grasshopper face staring into hers until the antennae stopped twitching.

The wasp was heading for the kitchen window, but it never stood a chance. A defensive sting was sidestepped quickly before powerful forelegs snatched it up, securing its head and stinger firmly, before violently eating the wasp's face. Its mouth worked like a wood chipper, mandibles crushing from the sides of the mantis's mouth as it chewed with the sound of blending flesh. An additional set of smaller arms from its midsection ripped into the wasp's abdomen, digging into its body until little fingers grabbed fistfuls of entrails. With its frontal lobe and eyes eaten away, the remainder of its head hung limp as the mantis continued to chew through its neck and into its body.

It ate until the stinger ceased its buzzing, and then it kept eating.

Meryl saw the gun poking out from underneath the couch and crawled to it. She kept her eyes on the praying mantis, its back turned in its feast, its wings fluttering in delight. She didn't dare make a sound. It hissed in between mouthfuls as she moved slowly, the butt of the gun just a few feet away. When she was close enough, she slowly pulled it towards her, dragging it through shards of glass and drywall clumps until her hand could curl around the grip. The gun felt heavier now, and her whole body ached. Her only relief was that the gun was still loaded.

Climbing quietly to her feet, Meryl shouldered the gun and crept through the living room. Ahead, the praying mantis chewed more slowly, the carcass nearly eaten in *half.* Insect blood collected in a growing pool at its feet, and the limbs—both human and not—reached lifelessly toward the floor.

Meryl considered running, but knew deep down this thing could just butcher her before she could even reach the driveway. But it had protected her, or at least appeared to. Would it turn on her next? Was it just taking out the competition to save the more savory prey for itself? Meryl knew she was well past the realm of real life. She didn't even think a SWAT team would stand against this thing.

A piece of glass cracked under her shoe, and the praying mantis turned to face her, the wasp corpse still cradled, its face covered with pulpy gore. She trained the gun on it and stepped forward, ready to give it both barrels. It stopped chewing slowly and let the corpse fall to the floor with a heavy squish. Meryl cleared her throat quietly before gripping the gun tightly.

"What the fuck do you want with me? What are you doing in my house?" she asked, feeling foolish for questioning the oversized bug. She expected it to rush her, fly across the house and decapitate her, but it just looked at her.

The praying mantis scanned the kitchen, as if to assess the damage. It was silent except for the occasional clack of the mandibles, working at the remaining flesh in its mouth. The second, smaller set of hands unclenched their fists and let go of the entrails they had been squeezing. Just as she was about to ask again, the creature did the last thing she expected it to do.

It raised its arms in surrender. Long, wicked fingers twitched at the end of its bladed arms, each dripping like well-used saw blades.

It took a step forward, and Meryl flinched, her finger hovering over the trigger. It chittered and bowed its head, covering its face with its claws. Aside from the spatter of bug insides, it was coated in what looked like dried human blood. Strands of flesh still clung to its chitin carapace. Whatever this thing was, it looked like it came from a man as well. Its long fingers pointed at her, almost nervously. One of them had something out of place, a shine that didn't belong to the rest of its disturbing form.

"What do you want from me? If you're gonna kill me, get it over with," Meryl said solemnly, the gun trembling in her hands. Whatever animosity it had moments ago seemed to be fading. It seemed like it wanted to come closer, but it was afraid to.

Meryl heard something squelch to her right. It was loud in the uncomfortable silence, and she noticed immediately that the grasshopper's body had moved. The lower half of it. She kept the gun trained on the mantis while side-eyeing it, her attention reluctantly shifting towards a sound that reminded her of worms after a heavy rain.

Something was working its way out of the severed waist. Something black.

It unspooled from the body part like it was birthed, a slimy coil that writhed as it untangled itself. One end probed through the debris, while the other plunged back into the lifeless lower half from which it came. A second later, the legs started to twitch.

There was something in the way the mysterious worm moved that made Meryl deeply uncomfortable. It reminded her of a horse-hair worm, but much larger. They were repulsive things, but generally small—but this one had the thickness of a steel cable and looked to be *growing*. She couldn't shake the feeling that things were about to get worse.

As she watched the worm, it paused and angled its exposed end towards her, as if it was looking up at her. Before she could react, it recoiled like a snake and shot towards her, wrapping around her waist.

She felt the rush of wind before she could swing the gun towards it, and saw the mantis had covered the distance in the blink of an eye, slashing with one of its bladed arms. The coil around her waist loosened immediately and fell to the floor, writhing at her feet like a snake without its head. She crushed it under her shoe, stomping it until it stopped moving.

The mantis had protected her again. It stood tall before her, its intimidating frame serving as a shield. She didn't understand why, but she felt the urge to aim the gun at it either way. Whatever was happening, she had somehow found an ally.

From between the spiked limbs of the mantis, Meryl watched the black threads multiply. They *spilled* from the grasshopper's legs, dozens of seeking hairs burrowing into the destroyed body parts, pulling them together awkwardly as it tried to assemble some kind of form, but wrongly placed. They wrapped and twisted around the pieces, splitting off until there were hundreds. The severed head fused into the mass like a shoulder and worked the bent legs like an arm. The tentacles hefted themselves up like a broken statue, a single torso and arm standing to face the mantis, until they were equal in height.

The mantis shrieked and pounced. The tentacled beast swung the grasshopper legs like a backhand, nearly knocking the mantis off its feet. As soon as Meryl raised the gun, a sentient cluster wrapped around the barrel and tried to wrestle it out of her hands. She pulled the trigger and blasted it into pieces before aiming into the concentrated mass and firing again. Her ears rang immediately, the sounds of squelching replaced by the deafening ring of tinnitus.

The shotgun appeared to do damage, but was soon repaired by more slimy tendrils. They bore into the eyes of the grasshopper's skull, drilling and replacing until they hollowed it out. The mantis charged it from the side and knocked it over, before raking it with a bladed arm. It tried to retaliate with its weaponized legs, but the mantis caught it in its mouth, chewing through it in seconds.

Meryl ejected the shells and pried two more from her pocket. She thumbed a cartridge into the bottom barrel, then the top. She snapped it shut and aimed at the struggle, and felt a bit of relief. With its superior strength and bladed arms, the mantis appeared to be winning. It looked like it would be over soon.

But when Meryl looked to the kitchen, her heart skipped a beat. The destroyed corpse of the wasp was getting up, a similar twist of disgusting hairs having expelled from it. Its wings were starting to beat, and the abdomen and stinger were brandished like a weapon. As she looked at it, she could see the buzzing.

"Look out!" Meryl shouted.

The wasp lurched from the kitchen, half flying, half galloping on its broken human hands. By the time it reached the living room, she realized it wasn't heading for the mantis; it was aiming for *her*.

The second she fired, it hit her with the force of a charging bull. Buckshot peppered the wall, and her teeth clacked painfully on her tongue as the monster tackled her into the corner of the room. An end table collapsed beneath them, and the weight of it crushed Meryl. She held the gun out defensively when the slimy hairs wrapped around it, materializing into fingers that tried to pull it away. Through the chaos, she heard the stinger, and it filled her with fear. A mass of hair jutted from its chest and held her in place, while the stinger arm arced over like a scorpion's tail.

With the sound of a power tool, it drifted towards her face, and with a sickening realization, Meryl saw how it intended to kill her. It was going to drill into her face, slowly. The stinger *whirred* as it got closer, rattling her teeth and skull as it reached between her eyes. She turned away from it and screamed, feeling the sensation of a thousand needles home in.

A shriek echoed across the room, just before clawed fingers burst through the writhing mass, and lifted it off of her. The mantis hefted the monster over its head and ripped it in half with a shrill cry, tossing the pieces to the floor next to the defeated grasshopper.

Meryl lay in place for a moment, blinking away another dance with death. Her nerves shot, and her heart beat so hard she thought it would explode.

The mantis looked tired. It stood hunched over the still writhing corpses, both arms dripping slime and bits of membrane. Meryl weakly picked herself up, and when it turned to face her, she could see it hadn't made it out entirely unscathed. Its armored skin was cracked in several places, and a few of the barbs on its limbs had broken away. It was missing one of its miniature arms on its abdomen, as if it had been twisted and torn off. It looked to be in pain, but remained standing nonetheless.

The sight upset Meryl, but she still brandished the gun cautiously. It still pointed in its direction, the remaining shell only a trigger pull away.

"Thank you..." Meryl breathed, leaning against the woodstove for support. Her ears rang and her body throbbed, and she felt like she was going to throw up again.

The mantis inched closer, as if concerned, its arms bent and motioning towards her. Meryl flinched away from it, and it shook its head slightly, its antennae twitching. Its crimson compound eyes stared ominously, and Meryl didn't exactly know what to do next. She couldn't exactly show up to the police station with it, gun in hand. As she ran through different scenarios, each more ridiculous than the last, she thought of what the officer had said before it attacked her.

We're not leaving until we see your husband.

She needed to find Wesley. There could be more of these things.

"We should go," Meryl said, addressing the large bug. It chittered for a moment, as if considering. Then, to her surprise, it nodded.

A deep *hum* erupted behind them, and the stinger burst from the mantis's chest.

"No!" Meryl cried as she watched it lift off the ground, a thick feeler of hair coiling around it like an anaconda. The mantis released a metallic wail as it was hefted into the air, and Meryl recoiled against the terror behind it.

The corpses had pulled themselves together, hundreds of puppeteering hairs stitching the vile mass into a fiendish chimera. An amalgamation of grasshopper, wasp, and human, all oozing strands that flicked like wagging tongues. It stood like a hound bearing its teeth, a single grasshopper leg bent at the rear, its front held up with human hands and broken fingers. The stinger now functioned as a tail, squeezing the mantis tightly as it balanced its new form.

A gurgling roar echoed from the mass, and its back bloomed disgustingly, revealing a single, infected eye. It stared at the mantis with unflinching hate.

Meryl aimed at the eye and fired. A severed leg shifted from the mass, just in time to shield itself from the blast. Buckshot punched into a booted foot, reducing it to a mess of rubber sole and bloodied bone.

Above, the mantis cut itself free, shredding the tail with its blades from the inside. The stinger wriggled free and slithered away, leaving a bleeding cavity in the chest of the mantis. Before it could recover it slithered around to strike again, the mangled wasp abdomen reared back like a cobra, lashing out like a cracking whip.

The mantis was too slow. The stinger pierced the armor of its shoulder quickly, and Meryl watched as the hardened flesh softened and burst like a popped cyst. The mantis's right arm fell lifelessly to the floor, the end sizzling like it was dipped in acid.

Meryl ejected the shells as the stinger soared towards the face of the mantis. With a last-second swipe, the mantis lopped it off at the neck, sending the still buzzing stinger squirming away. Meryl fumbled two shells home and snapped the gun shut before pinning the wasp appendage to the floor.

A single shot stopped it for good, reducing the horrible weapon to a mound of acrid yellow paste. The mantis looked momentarily at its ruined arm, its ominous eyes portraying no emotion.

The horsehair nest rumbled and blinked its grotesque eye, then charged. The mantis met it halfway but was overwhelmed immediately, and the two of them rocketed towards the far end of the living room. They collided with the woodstove with bone-breaking force, ripping it from its chimney with a loud crash as the nest's weight nearly consumed the mantis. Even as it was crushed, it kept its focus on Meryl, hissing as the many limbs pummeled it. It sawed through the human hands with its mandibles and slashed with its remaining arm, but it was clear the mantis stood no chance.

The mantis held it back long enough to speak—a raspy, barely human word.

Run.

It was giving her a chance to get away.

Meryl felt a lump in her throat as she backed away, the gun trembling in her hands. The slam that followed shook the entire house, the floorboards snapping beneath the mantis as the beast crushed it.

Meryl ran to the kitchen and found her keys immediately, the fob sticking out amongst the utensils and ruined cookware. Behind her, the monsters screamed, the deep gurgling roar followed by the shriek of the mantis. They were getting weaker. The nest was killing i t.

Clutching the fob in her hand, Meryl was overcome with guilt. When she turned to the door—her escape—she felt the dying cry of the mantis pierce her soul. It had sacrificed itself for her, and she didn't even know why.

She didn't have many shells left, and from what she had seen, they didn't seem to have much of an effect on it. She looked desperately around the kitchen for something that would work, something that it couldn't just brush off. If it made it out of her house alive, there was no telling how many more would fall victim to it, or what it was truly capable of if it wasn't stopped.

Meryl helplessly surveyed the collection of strewn drawers and broken cupboards, all the while haunted by the pained screeching. Standing amongst the wreckage, she found hope—in the form of peanut oil and a bundle of rags.

The gas burner clicked to life, and she tilted the jug carefully, igniting the many rags she stuffed in the neck of the multi-gallon jug. Healthy flames licked at the cloth as she lugged it to the kitchen doorway, where she saw the nest still looming, like a grizzly mauling its prey.

She lobbed the jug with all her might, and it landed on the monster's back, immediately sinking into the mess of sentient hairs. As the hulking eye turned its attention to her, she raised the shotgun and fired.

The jug erupted like a fountain, oil soaking deep into the folds of writhing worms. The fire that followed burned quickly and fiercely.

The beast roared as it went up in flames, shaking violently as withering worms tried to protect the eye. They smoldered and popped and melted like burning plastic, tortured faces and broken limbs lighting up at once like a walking bonfire. The nest squirmed and whined but could do nothing against the rising heat, shriveling away as the hateful eye tried to detach and escape, a last effort to save itself.

Just as its neck twisted to jettison it, a bladed arm pierced through the burning mass and stabbed it dead center of the inflamed pupil. A groan echoed through the house, and the monster thrashed, and the mantis's arm pulled free in a torrent of what looked like pus, blood, and tar. Its legs buckled, and it collapsed near the stairs, the flames spreading like waves in a burning ocean.

The eye looked at Meryl in despair, a silent plea for mercy even as she ejected her empties and loaded her last shell.

With a final trigger pull, it burst like a rotten watermelon. Through the explosion of discharge, a single organism tumbled and squirmed on the floor. An encapsulated cyst covered in veins and nerves. It beat like a living heart.

Meryl looked down on it with disgust before raising her shoe and crushing it with her heel. It ground into the floorboards with the sound of crunched carrots, and an inkling of a squeal distorting until it faded away. When it was silent, she kicked it into the flames, where it quickly shriveled like grisly cellophane.

The fire spread ravenously, bringing with it a wall of heat and billowing black smoke. The beast burned like a mound of tires, the multitude of species liquefying to molten ash.

Meryl scrambled through the room, shielding her eyes from the smog as she navigated the destruction. When she saw the mantis in the corner, she ran to it, pulling its disfigured frame from the rubble to safety. There wasn't much left of it, and the longer she looked, the worse the lump in her throat got.

Its hind legs were gone, crushed and claimed by the now-burning nest. Its torso was a pattern of cracks and splits, each bleeding an iridescent green that reminded her of the contents of a glowstick. The wings that hadn't been snapped off had melted in the fire. It only had one eye left, which remained locked on her as it hissed weakly.

"I'm sorry. I'm so sorry," she whispered, gently touching the smooth hide of its foreleg, slick and matted with gore.

With the house burning around her, she comforted it the best she could. Its compound eye watched her silently, and a glowing tear trickled from it. She took its hand in hers, remorse flooding her as she caressed its long, clawed fingers.

She felt the ring then, a circular band embedded in its flesh. She lingered on it, the cursive still legible despite the damage.

Forever and Always.

Tears welled in her eyes, and when she faced the mantis, it squeezed her hand softly.

Meryl sobbed—a bewildered, sorrowful whisper.

"Wesley?"

AFTERWORD

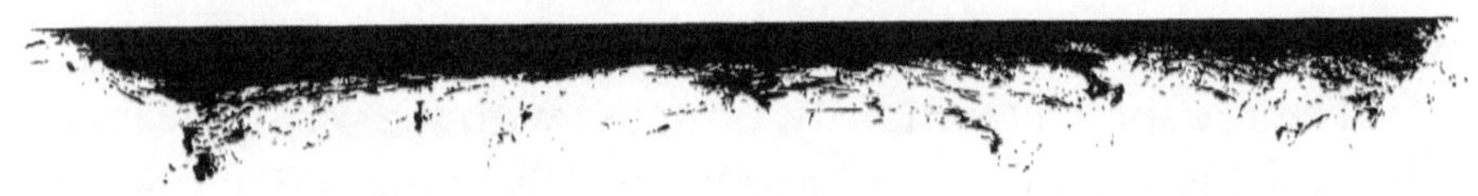

Old Man was my first short story. I was eighteen and just out of high school, packaging steel products, when I had the idea. I had first started writing in middle school—attempting embarrassing, nonsensical *Resident Evil* fan fiction, then again in high school, with a slightly more sensible zombie apocalypse story, although equally unrealistic and full of flaws.

I remember telling the guy next to me, a fifty-something mill worker who raised his eyebrows and probably didn't care whether I showed up for work the next day at all.

"Cool."

I wrote *Old Man* over three days, my first beginning, middle, and end. Loved it, thought it was the greatest thing. I remember printing some copies of it out and passing them around. Copies that would get lost, ruined, or thrown in the garbage. It didn't matter much to me one way or the other—I had written a *story*—one people seemed to find entertaining at least. My girlfriend—now wife—thought it was pretty cool too. Even painted a little picture for it.

An old man and a crow, an amber ring shared between them. A tale that would hang out in a folder for years, hidden away but not forgotten.

Five years later, I wrote *A Doctor's Visit*. Life had swept me up, and I found myself looking at the keyboard, wondering if I could do another. Maybe a little better this time, and undeniably horror. I wrote it in two days; two long stretches after night shifts, finished up right before a late-night hangout. My wife and friends all read it that night, each sitting at the computer in silence as they took in something that they hadn't necessarily planned to, but humored me nonetheless.

A man and some X-rays. A praying mantis. "Body horror". Hearing them discuss their favorite parts still sticks with me to this day, getting compliments on something that "was actually pretty fuckin' good". I planned on doing a sequel "someday".

Like the previous time, I didn't write again for a while, but I came back sooner this time. Determined to do another horror story, over an idea that floated around in my head for months. I had inherited my mother's collection of gargoyles, and was currently enamored with them. I wrote it over the course of a few days, testing the waters on writing violence and dialogue while trying to hone the realism of the interaction.

A stereotypical, albeit jaded, view of a rich man and his wallet, with a gargoyle somewhere in there.

I wouldn't write for years after that. It was one thing my friends and family would bring up from time to time. I thought about it a lot, but playing video games was a much easier way to pass the time. It wasn't until I had a few life-changing surgeries and spent a lot of time sitting around, did I feel the need to try and do something constructive with myself.

With a newfound love of synth/vaporwave music, I wrote for four days straight. Sulking in a basement, *Kavinsky* tracks on repeat. An alien abduction with a fresh take. An epic clash between young love and something from the stars.

It was corny and cringey. Bloated and redundant. But I was proud of it anyway, and when I let others read it, they seemed to enjoy it as well. And when it was all said and done, it sat in the same folder I created all those years ago. Hidden away, but not forgotten.

It was a long time before I wrote again after that. Thinking of the times I used to write and come up with these crazy stories that others found unique and descriptive. After years of looking back and regretting not doing more with something I enjoyed so much, I decided to give it a go again. For real this time. *Really* try to be a writer.

I have written over two hundred stories since then, with varying themes and lengths, and all kinds of different horrors. It's something I love wholeheartedly, writing tales to scare and maybe leave an impression once you've scrolled to the bottom.

The stories in this book lived like legends between my friends and family through the years. Inside jokes about a praying mantis, a funny remark when we saw a crow. They are important to me, and crucial in my growth as an author. Although they served as stepping stones in their time, I have since gone back and touched them up here and there, giving them the love they deserve today, no matter how painstaking the process was. They look pretty good now, I think, all dressed up.

And twelve years after writing *A Doctor's Visit,* it finally got the sequel it deserved.

I want to thank my friends and family for cheering me on through the up's and down's. I want to thank my wife, whom this book is dedicated to, for sticking by me and picking me up when I fall down. I would also like to thank *Velox Books* for delivering this in its best form.

Lastly, I would like to thank *you,* the reader, for taking the time to read this book. It might not be the craziest and biggest of them all, but it holds a special place in my heart. I hope you've enjoyed these stories as much as I've enjoyed writing them.

Until next time,
Jesse Pullins

MORE CHILLS FROM VELOX BOOKS

MORE CHILLS FROM VELOX BOOKS

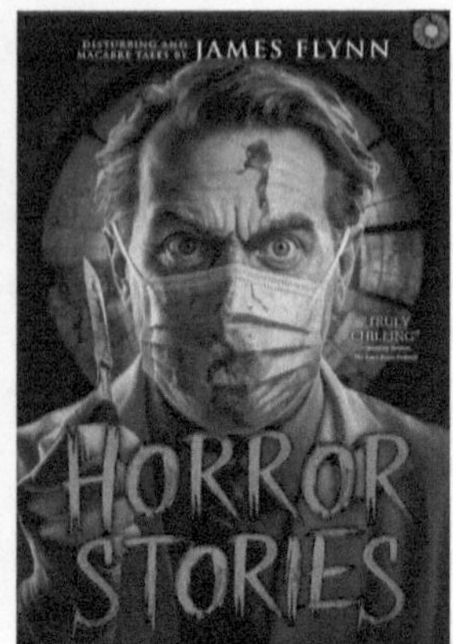

MORE CHILLS FROM VELOX BOOKS

MORE CHILLS FROM VELOX BOOKS